Saturdays in the City

Saturdays in the City

Ann Sharpless Bond

Illustrated by Leonard Shortall

Houghton Mifflin Company · Boston · 1979

Library of Congress Cataloging in Publication Data

Bond, Ann Sharpless.
Saturdays in the city.

SUMMARY: Two nine-year-old boys share a series of Saturday adventures in their city.
[1. City and town life – Fiction] I. Shortall, Leonard W. II. Title.
PZ7.B6366Sat [Fic] 79-11747

ISBN 0-395-28376-0

Printed in the United States of America.

M 10 9 8 7 6 5 4 3 2 1

For Larry 

CONTENTS

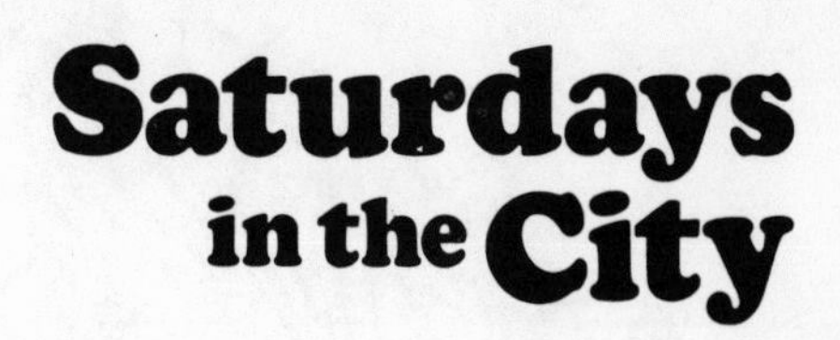
Saturdays
in the City

1. Rexy

Adam and Noah had spent a long time looking for dinosaurs. They usually did something together on Saturdays, and today they were dinosaur-hunting in the Museum of Natural History.

Their fourth-grade teacher, Miss Thomas, had said there was a Tyrannosaurus Rex in the museum. Noah especially liked this kind of dinosaur and was afraid that they had missed it.

"A dinosaur is too big to hide," said Adam. "We've just got to keep walking."

"That's all we've done," said Noah. "I bet we've walked five miles." He leaned over the rail that ringed the model Indian village and held up one foot at a time to rest it.

Hunched over like that, with his yellow hair falling over his eyes and his shirt tail out, he seemed smaller than he was. Adam, tall and neat in his new brown sweater and clean chinos, looked a lot older than his friend, even though they were the same age.

"We couldn't have walked five miles," said Adam. "The museum is only one block long. It runs between Forty-fourth and Forty-fifth streets."

"We keep walking in circles," said Noah. "We've come by this Indian village three times."

"That's because you have to look at everything," answered Adam. "How can we find the dinosaur if you have to look at everything?"

"Say, these Indians better watch out," said Noah. "They're just standing around planting corn and —"

"That's maize, not corn," said Adam.

"Well, they're not keeping a lookout," said Noah. "If I was an enemy tribe, I'd creep up behind that hill and sweep down on them. 'Bang, bang, bang!' "

"They didn't have guns, just bows and arrows," said Adam. "See, the bows and arrows are piled up beside that tepee."

"Well, my Indians have guns. They just raided some cowboys and took their guns." Hopping on one foot, Noah slid his arms along the rail. One hand shaded his eyes, and he whooped a little.

Adam felt uncomfortable when Noah pretended. Often as not, it led to trouble. He moved away.

Noah was now leaning far over the rail, using his finger for a gun: "Bang, bang, bang!" He slid and hopped faster and faster.

Adam saw a guard start toward Noah, but Adam reached his friend first and grabbed his gun hand. "How do we find Tyrannosaurus Rex?" he quickly asked the guard.

"Down the hall." The guard pointed. "Turn right, up the stairs. Go over to the other side of the building and take two left turns. You can't miss it."

"He doesn't know us," said Noah as they started off. "We can miss anything."

The boys took a lot of right turns and left turns and went up some stairs. They came to the cafeteria.

"I'm hungry," said Noah. "Maybe if we ate we could find that dinosaur."

Adam was hungry too, but just then Noah saw a small shop in front of the cafeteria.

"Look!" cried Noah. "Dinosaurs!" A box held tiny models of dinosaurs. A sign above it read SPECIAL 50¢.

Noah rooted around in the box until he found the one he wanted. "Here," he said in a hushed voice. "A real Tyrannosaurus Rex!"

"Well, it's nice," Adam admitted, "but it's not real."

"Feel how heavy it is," said Noah. "It's metal, not plastic."

"It's real metal, all right," said Adam. He saw the look on his friend's face as Noah held the little model. That look made him think of Christmas morning or hitting a home run.

"Now look here," he said sternly, "we only have one dollar between us. These days you can't buy much to eat for a dollar."

"I *need* Rexy," said Noah. "I'm not hungry anymore."

Later, inside the cafeteria, Adam sighed, broke his hamburger in half, and pushed one piece toward Noah.

The little dinosaur stood between them on the table as they ate. Eating didn't take long.

"Finding Rexy makes me feel lucky," said Noah. He ran his finger slowly from the dinosaur's small head along his bony back and tail.

"It makes me feel hungry," grumbled Adam.

"Now," said Noah, "maybe little Rexy will lead us to big Rexy. Let's go."

"He better not talk," said Adam. "No more of that two-rights-and-three-lefts-and-you-can't-miss-it stuff."

This time they tried not to walk around in circles, and Adam got Noah by everything but the whale.

The huge animal was in a room by itself. The walls were painted blue, and the whale hung from the ceiling on long wires. It seemed to float in water just above their heads.

"Wow!" said Noah. "Is it real?" He backed away a little.

"He's a model—he's not alive." Adam went

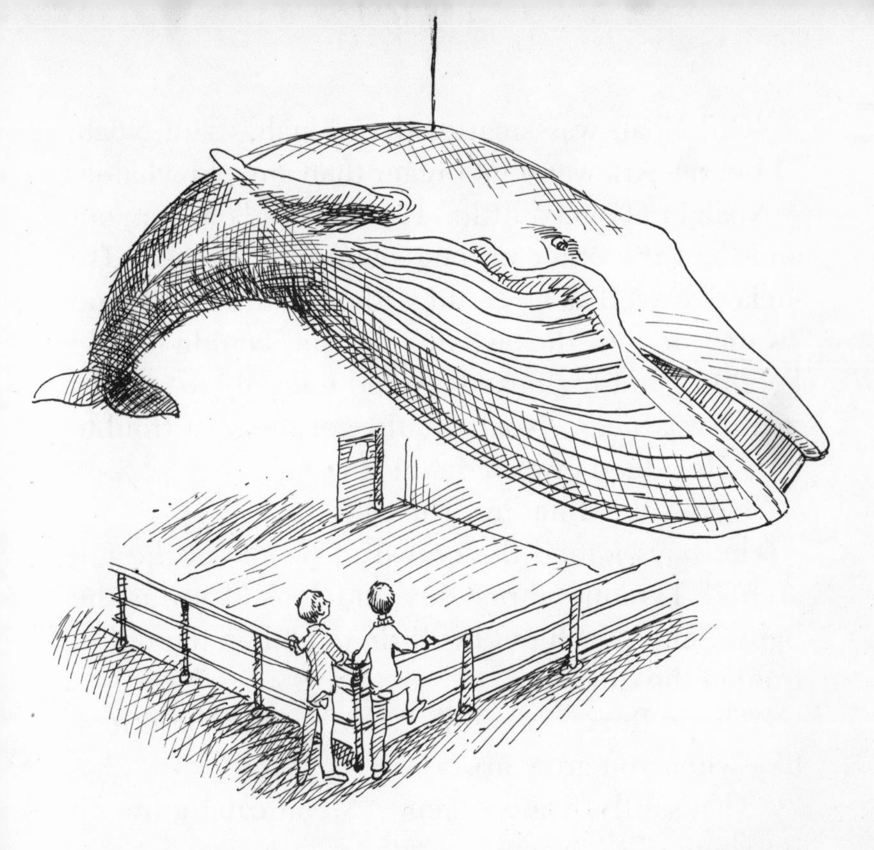

over and read the sign that told about the whale. “It’s a blue whale. It’s the biggest animal in the world.”

“He’d have to be big to swallow a man,” Noah said.

“No,” Adam said. “The sign says whales have a kind of strainer in their throats so they can only eat little fish.”

“What about Jonah?” asked Noah. “A whale ate him.”

“I forgot about Jonah,” Adam answered. “The sign doesn’t tell about him.”

"Old Noah was smarter than Jonah," said Noah. "I bet the Ark was a lot bigger than any old whale!"

Noah bent over a little. He stretched one arm out and then the other in long swimming strokes. He kicked as well as he could without falling over, and swam around the whale. Adam couldn't help laughing, but he looked around uneasily to see if a guard was near. Noah would get them in trouble yet. He edged toward the next room.

"Here's the dinosaur," he called.

The boys joined the crowd of people at the rail around Tyrannosaurus Rex and looked up at the bony giant. Noah put his little model on the rail in front of the dinosaur.

"There, Rexy," he said. "That's what you'll look like when you grow up."

"That's silly," said Adam. "Metal can't grow up into bones."

"I mean, what if," said Noah.

"The sign says that this dinosaur was king of them all. He was tougher and stronger than any of them!" Adam said.

"I know," said Noah. "That's why I like him. Now if my Rexy could grow up like that, I bet we could do anything!"

"Fifteen minutes until closing time," a guard called as he walked through the room.

Noah picked up Rexy and made the little dinosaur bow to the big one before he put it in his pocket.

The boys followed the other people into a dim hall that led to the main stairs. On each side of the hall were lighted windows, larger than most store windows. Inside were animals and trees and rocks arranged just as they would be in nature.

They stopped in front of the first window on the right. A large bear, taller than a man, stood on his hind legs.

"Wow!" said Noah. "He's not just bones. He's real."

"Sawdust," said Adam. "Just sawdust. Inside the bear skin, I mean."

"Those teeth aren't sawdust," Noah said. "Bet he could bite you."

"Bears don't bite you; they hug you. He could hug pretty hard, I guess," said Adam.

Noah put his little dinosaur on the rail in front of the window.

"If Rexy could grow," he said, "he'd be a lot bigger than that old bear."

"The trees are real," said Adam. "Hey, see the bird's nest up there?"

The boys stared into the lighted woods.

"I feel funny," said Noah. "I feel as if I'm really *in* there."

"The snake!" cried Adam. "See the snake on the log?"

"Closing time, all out!" boomed the loudspeaker above them.

Both boys jumped.

"The snake moved," said Noah.

"No, you moved," said Adam. "The snake is just full of sawdust, too. Come on, we have to go."

Noah slipped Rexy into his pocket and the boys followed the crowd to the stairs.

"What if that snake —" began Noah and then stopped. His hand was in his pants pocket. "Rexy's gone!" he cried. He turned to go back.

"Wait!" said Adam. "You can't go back! The museum's closing!"

"Maybe I left him on the rail in front of the bear," said Noah. "I can't leave Rexy!"

Adam looked down at his friend. Noah looked as though he was going to cry!

"You're silly, Noah," Adam began. "Rexy is just a —" But he stopped. Rexy was not just a toy. To Noah he wasn't. Rexy was special.

"OK," Adam said. "But we'll have to hurry."

They ran back down the hall. It seemed darker and longer now, without any people gathered in front of the windows.

Rexy was not on the rail in front of the bear, and he wasn't on the floor under the rail.

Noah got down on his hands and knees and felt under the rail near the window.

"Come on, hurry up," urged Adam.

Noah raised his head. Right in front of his nose, inside the glass, was Rexy.

"Adam!" he cried. "There he is! Inside, on the leaves."

"He couldn't get inside," Adam said. But there was the little dinosaur, lying on the dry leaves at the end of the log.

"He *is* magic!" whispered Noah.

Adam squatted down and looked at the bottom of the glass.

"The glass doesn't quite fit," he said. "Rexy must have fallen on the floor and been kicked inside."

Noah felt both of his pockets. "I must have put him in the wrong one," he said. "The one with a hole in it. We've got to rescue him!"

"Hey, you boys — out!" A guard stood at the far end of the hall.

Noah grabbed Adam's arm, and the boys ran out the door near them.

Ahead of them was the big dinosaur. To the right were stairs going up. They could hear heavy steps coming down them. The guard in back of them blew a whistle.

Noah pulled Adam away from the stairs. There was a small door on their left that had a sign reading NO ADMITTANCE.

Noah opened the door and the boys fell inside.

"Now we're in trouble," said Adam. "That sign means we're not allowed in here."

"I couldn't read the sign," said Noah.

"You could read the 'No,' " said Adam.

They were in a long, narrow, empty hall. The boys leaned against the wall and listened to the guards walking by.

"They aren't in the animal section," one guard said.

"They didn't go up those stairs," said the other guard. "I'll try the rockets. You try the birds."

"I can read that sign. It says 'Bear,' " whispered Noah, pointing to a small door opposite them.

Adam looked at the sign and thought for a while.

"You know," he said, "we came out of the animal hall and turned left. Then we came in this door on our left. So that door with the 'Bear' sign must be the back door of the bear window. There'd have to be a door so they could get all the stuff into the window."

"You mean Rexy is just inside that door?" asked Noah.

"I didn't mean —" Adam began, but Noah had pushed open the door.

They crept inside.

Dry leaves crunched under their feet. The small breeze from the open door stirred the branches of the trees a little. The sound and motion made everything seem alive.

Adam felt very strange. "We're in the woods," he whispered. "I mean we're inside them. We're — well — part of them!"

"Sure," said Noah. "I felt as though I was in here when I wasn't."

"I didn't," Adam said. His voice was odd because his throat was dry. "I was just *looking* in. I'd rather look in."

"The bear does look bigger from here," Noah said. "And hairier."

The boys stood very close together.

"See the squirrel going up the tree?" said Adam. "And there's a bird flying."

The small breeze died down as the door swung closed. The dry leaves were silent under their feet. The animals all seemed to be waiting for a signal to move: the squirrel to dash up the tree, the bear to lunge at the snake, the bird to fly to a treetop.

"I feel that something's about to happen," said Noah.

Adam felt that way, too. He also knew that if the squirrel as much as waved his tail, he, Adam, would begin to scream. He had begun to wonder what was real and what was not. "Maybe that something will be us leaving," he whispered. He turned eagerly toward the little door.

The door was not there. There was a mountain and a lot of trees, but no door.

Adam's hand felt wet as he rubbed it over his forehead.

"What if the door —" Noah began.

"Don't you dare 'what if,' " Adam said between his teeth. He forced himself to walk over to where the door should have been. The whole wall was painted! Of course! From outside the glass, the wall had been part of the scene — mountains and trees in the distance!

Adam ran his hands over the mountain. Yes, there was the crack of the door!

"Here's the door!" he cried with relief. "Let's get out!"

"But I haven't got Rexy yet," Noah said in alarm.

"Well, get him fast," said Adam.

"Come help me. He's in the leaves," Noah begged.

"You got us into this," said Adam. "You get him and I'll — I'll hold the door!"

Noah moved slowly toward the log.

Adam leaned against the little door. He felt a lot better having found it. "Say," he said, "that flying bird is just hanging from a wire!" He was glad he had seen the wire. Of course a stuffed bird couldn't fly in the air without a wire! Real things were real even on this side of the glass.

Noah stopped when he got near the bear.

"Adam," he said, "just stand in front of the bear, will you?"

"It's just an old stuffed bear," Adam said. "You can't be afraid of an old stuffed bear."

"It's the teeth," Noah said. "I don't like the teeth."

The bear stood on the right side, turned toward the window. The log lay on the left, and Rexy was nestled in the leaves on the far side of it.

Adam walked over and stood with his back to the bear so that Noah could hurry by it and get Rexy.

Adam watched Noah paw through the dry leaves. He glanced at the snake sunning itself on the log. It looked like a poisonous kind. He couldn't see the bear, but he knew that the great animal was right behind him. It made him feel small. He began to want to look around at the bear, but what if—?

"I've got Rexy," cried Noah, holding up the little dinosaur.

"Everybody out!" boomed a loud voice. A guard's heavy footsteps started down the hall from the far end.

Noah flattened himself behind the log.

Adam spun around toward the bear. But he had moved too fast. His leg hit the bear's and the huge animal swayed forward.

Adam flung his arms around the beast to keep it from falling. The bear was between him and the glass. He tried to hide his hands in the long hair. He buried his face in the bear's hairy back as footsteps drew nearer.

Adam felt a great thump, thump against his chest.

"It's full of sawdust," he said to himself. Thump. "A bear" — thump — "full of sawdust" — thump — "doesn't have a heart." Thump.

The guard hurried right by the bear window and out of the hall.

Adam let go of the bear very carefully and stag-

GRIZZLY BEAR

gered back. He could still feel the thump, thump.

He wiped his wet hands on his sweater. "I thought it was the bear's heart!"

"That's silly," said Noah, looking over the log. "You said he's just full of sawdust. He can't have a heart!"

"I'd like to see you hug him, if you know so much!" Adam said angrily.

"I don't know so much! You do!" Noah said. "You're always telling *me* what's real and what isn't!"

"Well, look. I stood in front of that old bear, didn't I?" Adam said.

"Sure you did," said Noah.

"And I found the door with that mountain and trees painted on it," said Adam.

"You found that old door, all right," said Noah.

"Well, let's go out that door right now," said Adam.

"I dropped Rexy when I heard the guard," said Noah. He began searching in the leaves again.

Adam's knees felt weak. He wanted to walk right out the door in the mountain and go home. He would too, as soon as his knees felt up to walking.

He stood with his back to the bear. Of course he was not afraid of it but, still, there was no use looking at it. He had not liked that "thump, thump" one little bit.

While he watched Noah messing in the leaves, he

thought he saw, out of the corner of his eye, the snake move a little along the log. "I know it didn't move," he thought. But he kept watching it.

The snake slid two inches forward on the log.

"The snake is sliding," Adam hissed. He stood very still. He knew that snakes strike at anything that moves.

"You said no 'what ifs,'" said Noah. "Here's Rexy. Let's go!"

At that moment, the snake slithered right off the log at Adam's feet.

Adam jumped backward and felt the bear's front legs around him. He let out a terrified yell and tried to jerk away from those clutching arms. His sweater caught in the bear's claws, and the bear and Adam fell over in a tangled, rolling heap.

Safe on the other side of the log, Noah clutched Rexy and watched the struggle between Adam and the bear. He was not at all sure who had started it. All along, he had not really trusted that bear.

When the two figures finally lay still, the bear on top of Adam, Noah began to yell.

"Help, help, oh help!" he hollered.

Heavy footsteps were already pounding down the small back hall, and soon the door in the mountain flew open.

Adam, his face pretty well pushed into the ground, dared to open his eyes. He saw a tiny animal about two feet from his nose. It had bright eyes and a long tail. It quickly turned and disappeared under the log.

He saw four large black shoes walking toward him and closed his eyes again.

In a very short time the guards marched the boys down the hall to a door marked DIRECTOR. Inside the door the four of them stood in front of the director's desk. Each boy had a guard's heavy hand on his shoulder.

One guard explained what had happened.

"We found them tearing the whole window apart! They knocked over the bear, threw the snake around, and messed up the leaves. I think they were going to steal the animals, but we got there just in time."

The director was a young man with a lot of yellow hair and dark-rimmed glasses.

"I can see that the boys caused a lot of excitement," he said. "But now that they're captured, why don't you guards stand over by the door so that they can't escape? Sit down, boys, and tell me how all this started."

"Well," Noah started, "this is Rexy." He put the little dinosaur on the director's desk. "He's special, you see."

"Yes, I can see that," said the director.

"Well," Noah went on, "he got inside the bear window and we had to rescue him."

One of the guards snorted and shifted his feet.

"He got *inside?* How?" asked the director.

"There's a space at the bottom of the glass on the log side of the window," said Adam. "Rexy fell through a hole in Noah's pocket and must have been kicked inside. That crack should be stuffed with something."

"Indeed it should," said the director. "No one ever noticed it before, even though some people walk by there every day." He shot a look at the guards. "But how did you get in?"

"Well, there's a little door," said Noah. "To a little hall."

"I know it well," said the director. "It says 'No Admittance.' "

"Noah isn't one of our best readers," said Adam.

"Just a minute," said the director. He found a pencil and paper and wrote, *Space under Bear Window*, then *Change sign from No Admittance to —* "Can you read 'Keep Out'?" he asked Noah.

When Noah nodded he wrote, *Keep Out*, then looked at Noah again and added, *Better lock too!*

"We were chasing them then," said the guard. "They were hiding in 'No Admittance.' "

"We hid because they were chasing us," said Adam. "We didn't know the door to the bear window was there. I wish Noah hadn't been able to read the sign 'Bear.' " He shivered. "It was awful in there."

"You were scared?" asked the director.

"Well," Adam said, "Noah's the one who likes to pretend. I like things to be real and stay real. I felt better when I found the door in the mountain and saw the wire holding up the bird. I know I knocked the bear over and he didn't hug me. But the snake *did* wiggle right off the log!"

Both the guards growled and shifted their feet.

"We try to make those scenes look real," said the director. "If you're inside where you shouldn't be, maybe you'd think you saw —"

Adam jumped up. "No," he said. "It was the mouse! I bet the mouse made that old snake fall off the log!"

"Mouse!" yelled the director. "There was a mouse in there?"

"I'm not scared of a mouse," said Noah in surprise.

"A mouse ran under the log when the guards came in," said Adam.

"*I'm* scared of a mouse," the director said, banging his desk. "Mice pull the stuffing out of our animals and can ruin our displays faster than anything else! If anyone has been bringing food into the galleries —" He glared at the guards.

"Not us, sir," said the guards. "Never."

The director pulled his list toward him. *Mouse traps,* he wrote, and underlined it twice. He threw the pencil down and looked at them.

"I'm sure that you're right about that mouse.

He's probably been digging under the log for some time, and it was about ready to roll a little. You two boys walking near it jarred it just enough to tip the snake overboard."

"I'm glad," said Adam. "I'm sorry you have mice if you don't want them, but I'm glad that the snake moved if I saw it move."

The director nodded. "You may be a scientist someday. What is your name?" he asked.

"Adam Tyler," said Adam. "Well, my real name is Christopher, but I have three older sisters and my father —"

"Called you Adam because you were the first boy," finished the director. "Your name?" he asked Noah.

"Noah Carter," said Noah. "You see, Noah is an old family name."

"Indeed it is," said the director. "It's a wonder we're not all called Noah."

"I'm really sorry that we ruined the bear window," Adam said. "We liked it very much from the other side of the glass."

"The other side of the glass is where you should have stayed," said the director severely. "However, the bear display is not ruined. We can stand up the bear and put the snake back on the log."

"We could help," said Noah.

"No, no, no," the director said quickly. "I have to keep my staff busy, you know." He tapped his list. "We'll follow up on your suggestions right away."

"We'll be back to look at the other animal windows," Noah said. "We missed most of them."

One guard rolled his eyes. The other guard held his head.

"You will? Well — yes — oh," said the director. "If you see anything wrong you'll come right to me, won't you? First thing, I mean. Before you *do* anything?"

"Sure," said both boys.

"Good," said the director. "The outside doors are locked now, so the guards will let you out. We wouldn't want them locked in here all night, would we?" He grinned at the guards.

"Say," began Noah as he followed Adam and the guards out of the office, "when it's dark in here at night, what if the animals —"

2. The Ark

"I'd like to be a sailor someday," said Adam. "I wish I could get on a ship and look around."

Adam and Noah were standing at the rail of the 34th Street Bridge one hot Saturday. Below them lay the great wharves which served the big ships that came upriver from the sea. The bridge marked the end of the voyage for the freighters and tankers, because the river was too shallow for them beyond the bridge.

"You can't," said Noah. "We can't even get on a wharf. Remember the man who hollered at us and shook his fist?"

"I'll think of something," said Adam. He was just tall enough to look down over the rail. "If we tied a rope to this rail, we could climb down and swim over to that ship."

Noah squatted down and put his head through the bars. Bits of garbage and pools of oil clung to the piers of the bridge. He shivered in spite of the heat.

"What would you do if you did get on the ship?" he asked.

"I'd think of something," Adam said.

"You better think of something else," Noah said. "I don't like this bridge much. Let's go."

"I bet you're scared of a little water," Adam jeered. "That's a good one. Someone named Noah scared of the water!"

"Who said I was scared?" Noah demanded.

"All right, then; we'll get on a boat somehow. I'll think of something," said Adam.

"I'm sick of you saying, 'I'll think of something,'" Noah growled. "Let's go!"

Adam looked hurt and moved along the rail. They were silent for a while as they watched a tug gently nudge a tanker up to a wharf.

Finally Noah became a monkey. Chattering "Chee-chee," he grabbed the top of the rail and, with knees bent, went swinging along until he bumped into Adam.

Adam laughed. "OK, we'll go. But let's look up the river first."

They waited for a break in the traffic and crossed to the other side of the bridge. Below them, tugboats pushed barges under the bridge to warehouses on either side of the river. Beyond, a few fishing boats moved lazily about.

Adam tried to think of some way of getting a ride on a tugboat. He was sick of looking at the river; he wanted to be on it. Noah didn't like to look right down at the water, so he looked far off to where the river turned westward in a big bend.

"Do you see some funny white things in the water up at the bend?" he asked.

Adam made his hands into binoculars and peered upriver.

"Sailboats!" he yelled. "Real sailboats! Let's go!"

"They don't look like sailboats," answered Noah. "They look more like sea gulls."

"That's because they're so far away," said Adam.

"A long, long way," complained Noah.

"Look," said Adam, "every time I think of something, you —"

"OK, OK," Noah said hastily. "I don't mind a walk, I guess."

They walked off the bridge and took a wide gravel path that ran along the river bank. It was a long hot walk, and Noah lagged behind, trying to kick stones into the river with a worn sneaker.

"Hurry up, can't you?" called Adam. "The sailboats might come ashore before we get there!"

"Look!" yelled Noah. "Field goal!" He aimed a stone toward the river, but it skidded off the side of his sneaker and just missed Adam.

"All right for you," said Adam. "I'm leaving."

He walked along faster. "Darn fool kid," he muttered. "I won't bother with him anymore. He'd have been sorry if that stone had hit me!"

Noah sat down and rubbed the side of his foot. He wondered about going home. Adam's back looked pretty mad.

Just then a young man with very long legs in white shorts came jogging along behind him.

Noah sprang up and jogged along beside him.

They jogged right by Adam.

Adam gave a snort of laughter and started to jog along on the other side of the young man. It wasn't long before Long Legs jogged right away from them.

The boys sat down to rest. "It was the shoes that made him go," said Noah. "He had real jogging shoes."

"He had real jogging legs, too," said Adam.

Pretty soon two young women came jogging slowly along. One was wearing red shorts and the other a blue jumpsuit.

"They won't get away from us," said Adam.

The boys let the women pass them, then jogged fast to catch up with them. They jogged along in back of the women for a while. Then Noah, his knees pumping high, started jogging around and around them. Adam thought this was a lot funnier than the women did. They kept up their steady pace.

Noah slapped his leg and yelled, "Giddy-up," and galloped and pranced faster and faster in a circle around the women. Adam started to gallop and circle the joggers in the opposite direction. This was fun until they bumped into each other right in front of the women and fell down on the hard gravel.

"Now *that* was funny," Red Shorts said as she jogged around the boys.

"We've jogged two miles," Jumpsuit said. "How far do you think you can go?"

"Two miles!" exclaimed Noah. "Where are they going?" He rolled on the ground, clutching his knee.

"Joggers don't care where they go," said Adam. "Just the number of miles."

The boys limped along a little farther, then stopped in amazement. They were delighted by the busy scene before them. The river was blue here and full of sailboats speeding back and forth in front of the small dock. A sign at the foot of the dock read RIVER SAILING CLUB, and triangular flags snapped in the breeze from the poles that held the sign.

"Is this the same river?" asked Noah in surprise.

"Gangway!" called two young men in bright swimming trunks as they went by the boys, carrying a sailboat onto the dock and slipping it into the water.

"That's the mast," said Adam as they watched the young men raise a tall pole.

"Sure, and that's the sail," said Noah scornfully as the white cloth was pulled up the mast. "Why does it have R Three on it?"

"This must be a racing club," explained Adam. "They have numbers so they can tell which boat is which when they're out on the water. See, all the boats are alike except for the numbers! I wish I could —"

"I know what you wish," said Noah. "Look!" he cried. "Those two boats are going to crash!"

Two boats just in front of the dock were speeding toward each other. At the last second Number 4's sail swung to the other side of the boat, and the boats skimmed by each other.

"See," said Adam, "you put the sail on the other side of the boat and that turns it."

"You know all about sailing already, don't you?" said Noah.

"No, but if I could go out on the dock and watch, I bet I'd learn," Adam replied.

The boys edged slowly to the dock.

A gray-haired man in white pants, blue jacket, and a hat with "Captain" on it was very busy there.

"Fifteen-minute gun coming up!" he yelled. "Cast off! Fasten that stay! No barging on the start! No luffing on the line!"

"What's he talking about?" asked Noah.

"I'm not sure yet," admitted Adam. "He's excited, all right. Sounds like my dad when he was packing the car to go to the shore that time."

Just as the boys had a foot on the first board of the dock, the captain saw them.

"Off! Off!" he shouted. "Clear the deck! Race time!"

Noah and Adam slowly retreated. "Every dock has a man to holler at us," grumbled Adam.

A small group of people had gathered on the shore to watch the start of the race. The boys moved along the bank of the river to get a better view of the boats.

A little finger of land stuck out into the river below the dock, and the boys waded through the high weeds and cattails that grew on it.

Adam bumped into something and almost fell down.

"Hey! Look at this old tub!" he cried.

An old wooden rowboat was pulled up on the bank, half-buried by the weeds. It had long since lost its paint, and two of its seats were broken.

"I suppose you want to ride in this, too," said Noah.

"Not me," said Adam. "It's even got a hole up here in the bow. Must be as old as the Ark."

Boom! came from the dock. The boys jumped and swung around to look at the end of the dock.

The busy captain stood with a string in his hand.

The string led to a little cannon fastened to the dock. A small cloud of smoke rose from the mouth of the cannon.

"Fifteen-minute gun," yelled the captain.

"Wow! Do you see that cannon?" cried Noah. "A real little cannon that works!"

"It's a beauty, all right," said Adam. "That old guy in the hat has all the fun."

"He won't let us near it, that's sure," said Noah. "He likes to boss people around. Let's go. Maybe we can pick up some joggers going back."

"Go?" exclaimed Adam. "Go, when the race is going to start?"

Noah looked out at the sailboats. "They're just going back and forth. They're not racing. Looks pretty silly to me."

"They haven't started yet," said Adam. "The captain yelled, 'Fifteen-minute gun!' The race must start in fifteen minutes."

"That's a long time to stand around waiting," said Noah. "I'm tired from all that jogging."

"Don't you want to see that cannon go off again?" Adam asked. "I bet there's another gun for the start."

"I do like the cannon," admitted Noah. "That's the best part of the race."

Adam leaned over the old rowboat and tested the back seat. "This one isn't broken. We can sit here and rest and watch that old guy fire the cannon."

Noah examined the rowboat carefully. It was pulled up on the land for almost its full length. Only the last two feet of it were in the water, and the water was only about a foot deep.

"Well," he said, "it would be nice to sit. The last part here is in the water. The boat couldn't — you know — *go* anywhere, could it?"

"Are you crazy?" asked Adam scornfully. "This piece of junk is grounded forever. Look, if you lie down on the bank with your toes in the water, would you go anywhere?"

The boys climbed in and sat with their backs to the land, watching the captain fussing with the little cannon.

"He's loading it for the next shot," said Adam.

It wasn't very comfortable in the rowboat. There wasn't enough room for their knees. The sailboats still sailed about but not in front of the boys. They all kept upriver from the dock.

"I wish they'd come closer," said Adam, standing up. "I'd like to see how they work them."

"I bet that old captain makes them stay over there," said Noah. "He's awfully bossy."

"I bet you're right," said Adam. "They have to stay over there until the cannon shoots again. They all have to start together."

"Sure, I'm right. Just ask old Noah the sailor."

"Here he goes again!" yelled Adam. Both boys jumped up as the captain picked up the string to the cannon and looked at a watch in his hands.

Boom! "Five-minute gun," he hollered, as the noise died away.

"Good," said Adam, sitting down again. "That means there'll be another gun in five minutes for the start."

Noah was restless, but he didn't want to leave until that last gun went off. They found that if they both slid to one side of the boat seat and then the other, the boat rocked a little. "Boats on land are sort of fun," said Noah. "We could pretend —"

"Here he goes!" shouted Adam. The captain again picked up the string and looked at his watch.

Both boys stood up and cheered as the *boom* rang over the water.

"That's funny," Noah said. "The cannon looks bigger now."

Adam turned and looked over his shoulder. The river bank was twenty feet away. He pushed Noah down onto the seat.

"We're afloat," he said. "We've started, too."

A small river current swung the rowboat around and carried it out beyond the dock.

Ten sailboats, their sails pulling hard, aimed directly at the old rowboat. The young men in the sailboats all yelled and shook their fists at the boys.

Adam and Noah sat like small stone statues, still facing backward, and waited for the crash.

At the last moment, sails swung wildly from one side of the boats to the other. Several sailboats bumped into each other, and there were cries of "Foul," "Luffing," as the fleet swept by them.

"Wow, oh wow," Adam said in a small voice. He looked at Noah. Noah looked very strange, as though he were frozen.

"I guess I was wrong about this boat not going anywhere," Adam said. "Maybe our wiggling around in this old tub made it slide into the water."

Noah was silent.

"It wasn't my fault," Adam protested. "You wanted to rock the boat, didn't you? Why don't you say something?"

"Let's go ashore." Noah's voice was faint.

"I'll think of something," Adam said. "Say, this is a rowboat! Maybe we could learn to row!"

The boys turned around very carefully so that they faced the bow. There were no oars in the boat.

"Well," Adam said, "it's kind of fun floating around, isn't it? The sailboats are gone. I guess we'll float to land sometime."

The breeze strengthened, and the boat began to rock a little. Noah slid off the seat and sat on the bottom of the boat.

"Now look here," Adam said angrily, "you're not going to be seasick, are you? You can't be seasick on a river!"

"Maybe I can," said Noah.

"Here we're having a real adventure," Adam complained, "and you're spoiling it all."

Adam sat hunched in the stern seat of the old rowboat and grumbled to himself. "If Noah weren't such a sissy we might be on a big freighter or at least a tugboat. Oh, no! He'd rather play horsey with the joggers! So now we're adrift in this leaky old tub."

Leaky was right. He realized that his feet were wet. A good three inches of water sloshed around in the bottom of the boat, and Noah was crunched down there, getting wet. Served him right!

The breeze from the east shore freshened and blew the boat farther toward the middle of the river. Adam looked first at one bank and then the other and realized that the river was a lot wider here than at the bridge. "Maybe a mile wide," he thought. That would be a long swim.

The boat rocked and swung and drifted for what seemed to be a very long time. Noah remained crouched and silent in the deepening water on the bottom of the boat. Adam looked down at his friend's bent head and felt angry and lonely. Where were Noah's jokes now? Why couldn't he pretend they were going to China or somewhere? Why was he acting like a dormouse?

A big wave hit the boat broadside and spilled more water on top of Noah, but he didn't seem to mind.

The next wave drove the boat against something solid, and Adam, turning quickly, saw that it was a buoy — a large barrel anchored to the bottom of the river with a pole and a flag waving from the top of it. He reached out and caught the pole.

"Hey, Noah," he said, nudging him with his foot. "I'll hang on here and maybe the wind will change and take us back to shore. See, we're straight off the dock!"

"Sure," said Noah very quietly. "Maybe we won't rock so much!"

Adam hung on to the pole and looked down the river. The sailboats looked pretty from here. Half of them were sailing toward one bank, and half of them were sailing toward the other bank.

"Guess they've given up racing," he said. "They're going in different directions."

Noah stirred. "It's wet down here. I'll come up on the seat if you hang on to that thing."

They sat on the seat with their feet ankle-deep in water and watched the sailboats.

"That's funny," said Adam. "Look, the ones that were going toward the opposite bank have turned around."

"And the ones that were going toward our bank have turned toward the opposite bank," said Noah.

Adam's arm got tired, hanging on to the buoy.

"It's not easy to hold this thing," he complained. "It keeps bobbing about, too."

"I feel better that at least we're somewhere," Noah said, "not just floating around."

Adam kept changing arms to hang on to the pole. It was hard work, but worth it now that Noah didn't look so much as though he was going to be seasick.

"The sailboats are getting a lot bigger," said Noah. "This old buoy isn't floating down toward them, is it?"

Adam glanced at the shore.

"No, we're still right off the dock," he said. "The boats are getting nearer to us."

Adam looked at the flag on the end of the pole. It was blowing straight down the river.

"The wind is blowing straight at the sailboats," he said. "Why don't they go backward?"

"Maybe because they keep going sideward," said Noah.

"Of course! They're zigzagging! With each zigzag they get closer to us. I think they're zigzagging to the buoy!"

Noah slipped down into the bottom of the boat again. The water was deeper there now. "Just keep hanging on," he said faintly.

Adam tightened his grip on the pole and faced the fleet bearing down on them. The zigzags got shorter and shorter as sails flipped from side to side with lightning speed. With each flip, the sailboats got closer to the rowboat and buoy. Adam could see the young men waving at him. The angry look on their faces made him decide not to wave back. Then he heard their shouts: "Go away! Clear the buoy!" Fear made him hang on harder with both

hands. He closed his eyes. The noise of the whoosh of boats, the yells of the men, the snap of sails, surrounded him.

One by one the sailboats rounded the buoy and the old rowboat, their sails whipping across the decks. There were yells of "Jibe" and "No luffing."

All but the last boat rounded the buoy. Its bow hit the stern of the rowboat, the sail flapped helplessly, and the sailboat turned over.

The blow loosened Adam's grip on the pole, and they were again adrift.

Noah peered over the side of the rowboat at the overturned boat and the bobbing heads of the young men in the water.

"They'll drown!" he gasped. "It's all our fault."

The young men shook their fists at the boys and yelled something rude.

"Nonsense," said Adam, "they can swim. No one goes out in a boat if they can't swim. Anyway, boats float even if they turn over, so they can hang on to the boat."

"Our boat looks as if it's going to sink," said Noah.

Adam looked down at the water in the boat. It had gotten a lot deeper and was now halfway up his legs. "Well, maybe a boat with a hole in it does sink," he admitted.

"Adam, I was the one who thought of rocking this old boat when it was on shore," Noah said in a small voice.

"I guess you were," agreed Adam.

"It's my fault," Noah said. "Don't feel bad when I —"

"When you what?" Adam asked.

"I can't swim," Noah said in a strangled voice.

A terrible kind of frozen pain hit Adam in his stomach. He sat hunched over staring at Noah's bent head. Noah might drown! Adam's mind began to work in odd jerks.

No wonder Noah didn't like looking over the bridge. No wonder he wouldn't even talk about swimming to the freighter.

And Adam had been mad at him! Noah could always make him forget that he was mad. He had turned into a monkey on the bridge, then a horse giddy-upping around the joggers.

"You can have my baseball mitt," said Noah.

Adam swallowed hard, but still his voice sounded strange.

"I can swim," he said. "I'll save you."

"No," said Noah, "you'll be lucky to save yourself."

Adam looked toward each distant shore, at the choppy waves. It was true. He might just make it alone.

"I'll think of something," Adam said fiercely. "Noah, I *will* think of something."

Noah gave a little groan.

Adam glared at the broken middle and front seats,

at a jet of water shooting through the hole in the bow, then down at the water in the boat creeping up to his knees.

"Get up on the seat beside me!" Adam suddenly ordered in a hard voice. "Take off your sneakers, quick!" He ripped off his own. A sneaker in each hand, he began to scoop up water and throw it overboard.

Without a word, Noah joined him. They bailed as fast as they could for a long, long time.

"You *did* think of something," Noah said, his voice sounding a bit stronger. "The water is going down a little."

Another jet of water shot through the hole in the bow as the boat bounced into a wave.

"Take off your socks," yelled Adam, pulling off his own and wringing them out. "Now, you're lighter than I am and we can't let that hole in the bow go under water for long. I'll get way in the back of this old Ark and you crawl up and push our socks in that hole. Hurry!"

Adam eased himself up on the back rim of the boat while Noah crawled through the water in the bottom of the rowboat and forced the ball of socks into the hole in the bow.

"Great!" said Adam. "You sure plugged up that hole!"

"It better work," said Noah. His voice was excited and strong.

They both bailed until their arms ached, and they they kept right on bailing. The water was now up to their shins.

They saw a small motorboat take off from the shore. They waved their sneakers at it, but it sped out toward the overturned sailboat.

The wind, coming in from the sea, had blown them a good way upriver beyond the dock but no nearer the shore.

Adam stopped bailing. "I'm going to pull out that broken middle seat," he said. "Maybe we can paddle with it."

He had to stand up and yank and pull to get the seat free, and the boat rocked hard. More water came over the sides. They bailed and bailed and bailed.

At last Adam tried to paddle with the broken board. By working very hard he could make the old rowboat turn around in a circle. Then he tried paddling first on one side then quickly on the other. He could keep the boat at least turned toward shore, but it didn't move forward.

"I'm going to get the front seat," cried Noah. He looked fine now, not seasick at all.

Adam watched as Noah stood up in the rocking boat and pulled and pushed to free the board. He longed to help him but did not dare to have two of them moving around in the boat at the same time.

After Noah freed the board, they had to bail

again. It took a great deal of bailing to get the water a few inches below their knees.

Although they had never paddled before, they learned very fast. Because Adam's board was longer and therefore gave a stronger stroke, the boat turned toward Noah's side when he paddled hard. He tried to pull the paddle back just enough to match Noah's stroke. They found that if they paddled together, they moved — ever so slowly, but moved — toward shore!

"Heave ho!" yelled Noah at each stroke. "Heave ho! Heave ho!"

"Sailing," sang Adam. "Sailing home again!"

Hoot. A blast from a horn stopped the paddles in midair.

They looked downriver. A large tug was steaming upstream, waves fanning out on either side behind it.

"I never saw a tug go so fast," said Noah.

"He's not towing anything," said Adam. "Maybe he's going home."

"He's blasting his horn at us," Noah said uneasily. "I think if we both keep on going, we'll — we'll meet!"

"You're right, but if we stay on this side of him we'll be caught by those waves he's making that are coming toward us. They'll push us out toward the middle again!"

"Look!" yelled Noah. "If we cross in front of

him, the waves from the other side of him will push us toward shore!"

"Sure," said Adam. "*If* we get across before he hits us!"

"Race you, old tugboat!" called Noah and dug his paddle into the water. Adam plunged his old board into the water, and they moved ahead a little faster than before. They didn't yell and they didn't sing. They paddled as hard as they could.

"If we're stuck on this side and those waves push us back," thought Adam, "we'll have to bail again. If we bail, we can't paddle. I'm not sure our arms will last forever."

The tugboat hooted twice. "It looks awfully big from here," Noah said with a gasp.

"He *might* try not to hit us," Adam said.

In grim silence the boys worked, their feet braced on the old boards under the water, their arms pulling and straining at the old seat-board paddles, which dipped and pulled exactly together.

The rowboat and the tug arrived at the same spot on the river at almost the same moment. The boys looked up at the gray bow looming above them. Then the tug, with a jerk of its steering wheel, pulled off and went behind them.

The paddles across their knees, they slumped over them, breathing hard. The first of the waves made by the tug raised the stern of the boat and shot it forward.

They started to laugh, and as each wave in turn pushed them toward shore they laughed harder. Adam almost fell overboard, he laughed so hard.

"Stop luffing!" yelled Noah, and they laughed harder still.

Finally, as the waves from the tug were spent, the shore seemed within reach. Grabbing their paddles, they dipped and pulled with happy, strong strokes. It was as if their arms had never ached from bailing, never ached from paddling.

A point of land reached out into the water a hundred yards upriver from the dock. Pretty soon the old rowboat was just below this point, and the waves and wind were quiet here. The boys stopped paddling a few feet from land.

"Adam, you sure thought of something," Noah said. "You thought of a lot of things."

"Didn't want your old baseball mitt anyway," Adam said, punching Noah lightly on the shoulder.

"It's better than yours," Noah said, punching back.

"Well, I guess we better take this old tub back to the sailing club," Adam said.

Noah looked down toward the dock. Sailors were busy there. All the boats had finished the race.

"I'm not sure," Noah said. "They were pretty mad at us."

While they were talking, a small inshore current caught the boat and floated it gently down toward the dock.

Adam dipped his old seat board in the water. "Look!" he cried. "It touches bottom! We can walk to land!"

"It would be a long walk home," said Noah. "Might as well drift down farther, as long as we don't have to paddle."

As the rowboat drew near the club, the sailors stopped fussing with their boats and watched them come.

When they drew nearer, they saw the busy captain shaking his fist at them.

"Go away," he called out. "Far away."

"Don't you want your old tub?" yelled Adam.

"It's not ours!" the captain said. "Keep going!"

"Look," cried Noah. "They're going to shoot us!"

A young sailor had grabbed the string to the little cannon. He was laughing and waving.

"Don't be silly," said Adam. "It only shoots blanks!"

Just as the Ark drifted past the end of the dock a *boom* rang over the water.

"Finish gun!" yelled the sailors, laughing.

The captain shook his fist.

"My, that was nice of them," said Noah. "They shot that old cannon just for us!"

"Sure," said Adam. "But I think we better keep going."

The current kept them close to shore as they glided along. Adam tested with his paddle to make sure the water was shallow. "I can't wait to get out of this thing," he said.

"It's a pretty good old Ark," said Noah.

"Good?" cried Adam. "Are you crazy?"

"It got us here, didn't it?" demanded Noah.

"*We* got us here," said Adam grimly.

Pretty soon the rowboat hit an underwater rock, and the bow lurched into the river bank.

"We get out here," said Adam firmly.

The boys jumped out on the shore, and Adam sat down suddenly. "My legs feel weak," he said.

"That's funny," said Noah. "You didn't bail or paddle with them. You rest, then we can pull the Ark up in the weeds here." He looked around. A warehouse stood half a block away. "No one will bother it here."

"Pull it up?" Adam groaned. "Why should we? I never want to see it again!"

"You don't want it to float around bumping into other boats, do you?" asked Noah. "That wouldn't be right."

"Well, it's heavy," said Adam. "How can we pull it up?"

"You sit on the back," Noah said. "Then the bow will go up a bit. You push with your paddle and I'll pull the bow."

"You know all about boats all of a sudden," Adam grumbled.

It wasn't easy, and finally they both had to wade

into the water to push. They gathered mud and put it under the boat to make it slide. And at last they got it up into the weeds.

Noah pulled the socks out of the hole and examined it. "We could fix that hole," he said, handing Adam his socks. They were almost clean from the water.

"You *are* crazy," Adam said.

"And paint the name 'The Ark' here," Noah said, patting the bow. "And buy some oars."

"Noah, you almost drowned!" Adam cried, his voice shaking.

"*I've* thought of something," Noah said. "I'm going to learn to swim! Every day I'm going to the 'Y' until I can swim!"

3. The Octopus

One cold, wet Saturday Adam and Noah joined the line in front of the local movie house. The sign above them read, SEE THE HORRIBLE GIANT OCTOPUS. A young man in a faded green jacket was in line in front of them. He looked very tall in the line of boys and girls waiting for the box office to open.

"I hope he doesn't know that there's any love stuff in this picture," said Adam to Noah, nodding at the young man. "I don't want to spend my money on love stuff."

"There might be," said Noah. "Here come Bootsy and Anne. Girls like that stuff."

Adam was careful not to look around, but Noah greeted Anne and Bootsy, though not the two other girls with them. He never could remember their names. They just looked like girls to him.

"Aren't you going to say hello to your girl friend?" he asked Adam in too loud a voice.

MONSTER THRILL
COMING NEXT WEEK
DARK MOON
CORN

"Shut up," growled Adam, hunching his shoulders.

"You said her hair —" began Noah, but a police car, siren screaming, shot by the movie house and stopped in the middle of the next block, drowning out his voice.

"Wow!" said Adam. "Maybe we'd better go and see what's happening. It might be better than this octopus thing."

The young man in the green jacket turned around. "No, kid," he said. "It's just one of those burglar alarms going off by mistake. They do it all the time. I heard it as I went by there."

"We can't go," said Noah. "The line's moving. I don't see why you always get excited by a siren."

"Well, it could mean a real story. Not some dumb thing made up about an octopus." Adam edged out of line.

"Give me your money and I'll get the tickets," Noah said quickly. "You go get the popcorn before the rush starts."

"No," said Adam. "It's your turn to buy the popcorn. I'll get the tickets."

"How about that soda I bought you last week?" demanded Noah. "And the candy bar on Thursday?"

"You were paying me back for the hamburger in the Museum of Natural History," Adam pointed out.

Noah gave up and, as Adam's turn came to buy tickets, he crossed over to the popcorn machine.

The young man in the jacket was ahead of him, and Mr. Warner was leaning against the wall. Mr. Warner had been a policeman once, but now that he was retired the movie house hired him for the Saturday matinee, to make sure that the kids behaved themselves.

"You're a little old for these pictures, aren't you?" he asked the young man.

"Oh, anything for a laugh," the young man said.

"Hi, Noah," Mr. Warner said, greeting him. "This time you better be nice and quiet and not get scared by the picture and start to holler."

"Look here, Mr. Warner, that was two years ago. I was just a little kid then."

"You're not much bigger now. Be careful the octopus doesn't grab you." Mr. Warner grinned at the young man.

The young man laughed. "Here, Noah. I'll treat you." He put two quarters in the slot and got two boxes of popcorn. He gave one to Noah.

"Thanks a lot!" said Noah. "That's great of you! Look, Adam," he cried as Adam came over with the tickets. "We got a free box!"

"Good," Adam said. "Put your quarter away and you can treat next time."

"What do you mean? I treated this time!" cried Noah.

"If you didn't pay, you didn't treat," insisted Adam.

The boys continued to argue in the lobby. They

stood at the rail watching the lighted theater start to fill. There was a good deal of milling around as each small group chose its seats.

Finally, Adam led Noah, still arguing, down the aisle and picked out two seats in the middle. They were right behind Anne and Bootsy and their friends.

"Of all the seats to pick!" began Noah. "And you said you don't have a girl —" Adam nudged Noah sharply in the ribs.

"You know I can't see right over someone," Noah growled. "Look at all the seats we could sit in with no one in front of us!"

"We'll count this popcorn as your treat," said Adam.

Noah was speechless. It wasn't like Adam to give in so easily. He felt trapped. He practiced craning his head around Bootsy's pigtails to see how much of the screen he could see. He could tell that he would have to wobble this way and that and then see only half of the screen at a time. Still, a quarter was a quarter to the good. He turned around to see how many empty seats there were, and there were a great many. The young man was sitting right in back of him.

"Don't let the octopus get that popcorn," the young man said.

"Sure won't," Noah replied. "Thanks again."

The girls were whispering and giggling in front of them.

"I only said," Adam whispered to Noah, "that Anne's hair is all smooth."

"Sure it is," Noah whispered back. "But Bootsy can throw a ball just like a boy. She tackles hard, too."

"But she doesn't look *clean.* All shiny and clean."

"Well, you can't look clean when you play football, can you?" protested Noah.

"What are the names of the other ones?" Adam asked. "The ones that look alike."

"They don't look alike," said Noah. "They just look like girls. You know the way most girls look; you can't tell them apart."

"I think these two are called Helen or Ellen or Nelly or something," Adam said.

"Or Melly or Telly or Belly." Noah was laughing hard.

The four girls wagged their heads from side to side in disapproval. Bootsy's pigtails whipped back and forth. Anne's hair swung gracefully, and the other two girls' just flopped.

"Isn't this picture ever going to begin?" complained Anne.

Noah looked at his birthday watch on his wrist. "Two minutes before two o'clock," he said.

Mr. Warner walked down one aisle, across the front, and up the other, glancing at the audience.

"He's not after me already, is he?" asked Noah

uneasily. "Just for laughing before the picture begins?"

He looked around and saw Mr. Warner go back into the lobby. The young man in back of them was scrunched down in his seat.

The house lights dimmed, and the picture began.

On the screen an oil rig was drilling just off a sandy beach. Suddenly the cap blew off a large pipe, and a stream of black oil shot into the air. The men on the rig rushed around to recap it.

The stream changed to bright green. The green liquid shot high into the air and began to grow. It swelled and swelled, and long arms shot out of the mass. It became a huge green octopus. It floated in the air for a moment, then plunged down on the rig, grabbed a man in each of its eight long arms, and dashed the men into the sea.

The audience gasped.

"Good," said Adam. "I like some action."

"Sure," said Noah around a mouthful of popcorn. "No love stuff today."

There was a girl, though; she was wading in the water with her brother, and the octopus saw them. She had very long yellow hair, and she was so beautiful that Adam groaned a little and the young man behind them whistled softly between his teeth.

The octopus headed for the beach. Its huge body floated just above the water, and it paddled swiftly with pink hands at the ends of its long green arms.

The girl tried to run through the water to the beach. Her long hair streamed out in back of her. It rippled and floated and bounced and swirled.

The four girls in front of Adam and Noah huddled together, squealing a little. Noah had a good view of the screen, now, over Bootsy's right shoulder. He leaned forward, holding the box of popcorn.

A slimy pink hand on the end of a long arm reached out for the yellow hair.

At that moment, a wet, cold object hit Noah in the back of the head and knocked the popcorn box out of his hand.

Adam grabbed the box in one hand as it flew by him. He tried to clap his other hand over Noah's mouth before he yelled, but he was too late.

Fortunately, Noah's mouth was full of popcorn and his yell was not very loud. It ended in a choke and a gurgle. He had jumped up, however, and in a matter of seconds Mr. Warner was standing in the aisle, glaring at him.

Adam had his arm firmly around Noah's shaking shoulders, and Noah managed to choke rather quietly.

Mr. Warner shook his finger at Noah and left.

Adam turned around to face the young man. "What are you trying to do," he demanded, "get us thrown out?"

The young man was scrunched farther down in his seat; he seemed very upset.

"Sorry, sorry kid," he whispered. "I was just taking off my jacket."

When Noah recovered, he wanted to know what had happened in the movie.

On the screen, the boy and girl were running down a street.

"Didn't the octopus get her?" he asked. He sounded disappointed.

"How do I know?" demanded Adam. "With you jumping around and yelling, I missed it too. This is no way to see a movie."

"Shh," Bootsy and Anne said.

"That octopus was really moving," Noah whispered. "He should have them both by now."

One of the look-alike girls turned around and whispered, "The octopus only goes fast over water, where it can paddle. On the land it only oozes."

"Gee, thanks," said Adam. "I'd like to see it ooze."

Up on the screen, the girl and her brother stopped a lady with some packages and told her about the octopus.

"Don't spread silly stories," she told them.

A policeman who was directing traffic said, "Run along kids. I'm busy."

"Just like grownups," muttered Adam. "They don't listen."

The girl and her brother went home. Their house was set back a little from a cliff that overlooked the beach. They sat on the porch drinking sodas, which made Adam thirsty.

"I guess the octopus has gone back to the sea," the brother said.

At that moment a thin green line appeared at the top of the cliff. Slowly, slowly, it moved over the top until the whole huge monster came into view.

The boy and girl jumped up and leaned over the rail watching it.

"Maybe it'll get her now," Noah said.

"Shh," said Bootsy.

A high wall ran a little in back of the cliff. The octopus oozed up the wall and slowly began to flow over it.

"Say, that thing can really ooze," said Adam.

"It's as big as a truck," said Noah.

The boy and girl began looking for things to throw at the monster. The boy picked up a large can of yellow paint from the corner of the porch and threw it as hard as he could. It bounced once, and the lid came off.

The octopus oozed over to the spilled paint and began to eat it. Gradually, its green color faded, and the octopus became bright yellow. It began to make deep glugging noises.

The girl got a large box of soap powder and threw it at the octopus. The monster swallowed it whole, as if it were a pill. Then it gave a big glug, and yellow soap bubbles began to gurgle up from its mouth. Bubbles exploded all over the creature and flew into the air. More and more came popping out.

The audience loved it and rocked with laughter.

Adam laughed so hard that he dropped the popcorn box. He fished around on the floor and found a box. As he sat up, he felt a hand grab his shoe and then let go. He jerked his knee up hard and it crashed against the back of Anne's seat. She turned and gave him a dirty look.

Adam felt a chill of fear. Of course he wasn't afraid of the octopus's pink hands, but he thought a hand had grabbed his shoe.

"Come on, let's move," he whispered hoarsely.

"Not now. The octopus is moving again," Noah said. "Maybe it can ooze right up on the porch!"

"We'll get a seat with no one in front of us," Adam said. "You'll be able to see better." He got up and began to squeeze by the two kids next to the aisle. He glanced back; the young man was no longer there.

Noah followed, trying not to take his eyes from the octopus.

They settled in seats across the aisle, a few rows nearer the screen, with no one in front or in back of them.

Noah reached for the popcorn box and dug his hand in. "There's hardly any left," he said. "You must have spilled some."

Adam took the last handful and crammed it into

his mouth. Something hard was in the middle of the mouthful. He chewed very carefully and managed to get the hard object out.

"Hey, look, Noah. I got a prize!" He held up a ring.

Noah looked at the ring in the dim light. "You got a prize and I'm the one who got the box. It's not fair."

"What do you want a diamond ring for?" Adam asked.

"Why do you want it? I bet you'll give it to Anne, won't you!" said Noah.

"Well, it would look nice on her. Bootsy would probably put it through her nose!" Adam said.

"Look," said Noah, "the octopus is going to eat that girl's sweater now. I bet it turns blue!"

"They don't put prizes in popcorn boxes," Adam said. "There's something fishy here."

"Look, it did turn blue," Noah said. "Well, I guess an octopus is fishy."

"Noah, what stores are there down the street?" Adam asked.

"Shut up, can't you? The octopus is almost on the porch."

"This might be important," said Adam. "After the drug store, what's next?"

"A food store and a shoe store," Noah said.

"And a jewelry store before the shoe store, right?" Adam asked.

"Sure," said Noah. "I forgot the jewelry store. They're going to throw a big bottle of catsup! Now the octopus will turn red!"

"Red and blue make purple," Adam said. "Noah, let me see your watch a minute."

"What's the matter with you? Don't you want to see the picture?" Noah complained.

"Just put your wrist on the seat arm," Adam said. "You don't have to take the watch off. You can go on looking at the picture."

Adam took the ring and rubbed it hard on the glass of Noah's watch. He quickly felt the glass. It had a deep scratch.

"You've ruined my watch," Noah said, surprised. "Adam, how could you do it?"

"I didn't hurt your watch. Just scratched the glass. Listen, Noah." He leaned over and whispered in Noah's ear, "There's a real diamond in this ring!"

"You're nuts," said Noah. "First you say there are no prizes in popcorn boxes but there's one in our box. Then you say the ring has a real diamond in it. What's wrong with you?"

"Well, did we ever get a prize in a box?" Adam asked. "We've eaten an awful lot of popcorn. Did you ever hear of anyone getting a prize?"

"That's true," said Noah. "But you didn't have to ruin my watch!"

"Just the glass," said Adam. "Only real diamonds

scratch glass. I had to prove it." He jammed the ring on his thumb where it stuck fast.

Noah stopped watching the purple monster. He leaned over and whispered in Adam's ear, "Don't give a real diamond to Anne. You might have to marry her or something!"

"Look Noah, I can't give this ring away. It's been stolen. We might be in trouble!"

Noah forgot the purple octopus. "The burglar alarm we heard might have been in the jewelry store?" he asked.

"Yes, it could have been," said Adam. "That man in the jacket said it went off by mistake, but maybe it didn't. Maybe he was lying."

"He was nice, though. He bought the popcorn for me. Say, you don't think he put the ring in my box, do you?"

"How did he happen to buy it for you?"

"Well, Mr. Warner was asking him if he liked movies for kids and he said, yes he did. I came along and he knew my name and said he'd treat me."

"Did Mr. Warner call you by name first?" Adam asked.

"I guess he did," said Noah. "And made some dumb remark about how small I am. I wish people wouldn't—"

"Could the man have put the ring in your box?"

Noah thought for a minute. "No," he said. "He

just got the box out of the machine and gave it to me. If he's a bad guy, why did he buy it for me?"

"Maybe to make Mr. Warner think that he was a good guy," said Adam. "I bet he wanted to hide in the theater."

"I feel creepy, thinking he's still in here," said Noah. "I hope he left."

"I've still got the ring," said Adam. "What if they think I stole it?"

"Mr. Warner is all right," said Noah. "You can tell him what happened."

"But what did happen?" asked Adam. "How did I get this ring in my mouth?"

"Say, he hit me with his jacket! Maybe he meant to," said Noah.

"He looked very upset afterward," said Adam. "I thought he looked scared. I bet it was because Mr. Warner came down to see what was the matter."

"I dropped the popcorn box then," said Noah. "Maybe he got it and —"

"No, I caught it," said Adam.

They watched the screen again. The octopus had found a bag of grass seed.

"But I dropped the box after that!" exclaimed Adam. "And you thought there was too little left in it! I bet that was *his* box!"

"Maybe he put the ring in his box and hid it under my seat when Mr. Warner came down the aisle to bawl me out," said Noah. "You picked up his box."

"Yes, it could have happened like that," said Adam. "I felt a hand on my shoe. I bet he was reaching for his box!"

"You better go and tell Mr. Warner right now," said Noah. "The picture is almost over, and I don't like the idea of a robber waiting to follow us when we leave."

Adam thought for a while. "You know how grownups don't really listen," he said. "Our story is hard to explain. It's sort of mixed up. And how do I get this thing off my thumb?"

Noah had been looking around the theater. "He's back there," he whispered.

Adam peered around. Across the aisle, a few rows in back of them, the young man was sitting right in back of Anne. The two seats between him and the aisle were empty.

The boys stared at the screen, but the octopus wasn't scary anymore.

"You better run right back and explain it to Mr. Warner," Noah finally said.

"What if the man in the jacket tackles me and — well — cuts off my thumb to get the ring?" Adam demanded.

"He wouldn't do that!" exclaimed Noah.

"It's all very well for you to talk; it isn't your thumb," replied Adam.

The octopus seemed to be growing grass all over himself, and the audience, except for Noah and Adam, were delighted.

"Maybe we just made this up." Noah sounded hopeful. "Maybe that old burglar alarm did go off by mistake. Maybe that jacket man does like kid movies and isn't hiding in here and —"

"We didn't make up the ring," said Adam. "I didn't make up that diamonds cut glass. I read about that once."

"Say," said Noah, looking at the screen. "The boy is running for the lawn mower. He'll mow down the octopus and that will be the end of the picture. We better do something or that old robber will follow us!"

"Or he'll escape," muttered Adam. "I'm mad that he's ruined the picture for us. I wish we could prove he stole this ring!"

While the boy on the screen was having a hard time starting the lawn mower, Adam was thinking.

"If we drop our box of popcorn and he picks it up, then we'd know he'd put the ring in it and is looking for it."

"But the box is empty," said Noah.

"He doesn't know that. I'll close it up and drop it as I go by him. If he grabs it, we'll know he's looking for the ring."

"Maybe he'll just be looking for more popcorn," Noah objected.

"OK," said Adam. "I'll step on the box so it looks

like a used-up one." He crunched it under his foot. "Now even you wouldn't pick this up looking for popcorn, would you?"

"No," said Noah. "I don't think I even like popcorn anymore."

The boy on the screen had gotten the lawn mower started. The octopus was still growing grass in front of the porch.

"I guess we'll have to do something now," said Adam. "I'll go first and drop the box as I go by him. You come along in back of me and see if he picks it up."

"What should I do if he does pick it up?" asked Noah.

"Just run out to the lobby and we'll tell Mr. Warner. He was a cop — he'll know what to do."

Adam walked quickly up the aisle, and just opposite the young man he dropped the box and started to run toward the lobby.

Noah, following him, saw the young man quickly move to the empty seat on the aisle and reach out for the box.

Noah was in such a hurry to run after Adam that he stumbled. One foot shot out, and he kicked the box straight under the row where the four girls were sitting.

The young man dived under the seats in front of him, his hands grabbing at the skidding box.

Anne sprang to her feet with a loud scream.

Bootsy leaped up with a loud yell. The other two

girls followed them, hollering with all their might.

Noah stood still, stunned by what he had done.

The row of people in front of the girls turned to see what had happened. The sight of the four screaming faces set them off, too. They joined in the yelling.

In seconds, the noise spread through the crowd like a wave. It joined the sounds from the screen of the lawn mower chopping up the octopus.

Adam had stopped running at the first scream. He saw Anne's head clearly in front of the lighted screen. He remembered the hand grabbing at his ankle and knew at once what had happened. The robber had grabbed Anne's ankle while reaching for the box.

He ran into the lobby and bumped into Mr. Warner.

"He's grabbing Anne! He robbed the jewelry store! Here's the ring!" Adam held up his thumb.

Mr. Warner stared at Adam. Then the waves of noise from inside rolled out into the lobby. He pushed open the street door and, taking a whistle from his shirt pocket, blew three sharp blasts.

Then, with Adam at his heels, he crossed the lobby into the theater.

Inside the theater the boys and girls crowded the aisles, and Noah couldn't see the young man or the girls. He wished that Mr. Warner and Adam would hurry. He stood up on a seat and caught sight of

Anne and Helen or Ellen pushing their way into the aisle. Bootsy was not with them. The young man had disappeared.

Then he saw Bootsy's pigtails leaping into the air above the back of her seat.

Noah pushed his way across the aisle and into the row in back of Bootsy. He leaned over to see what she was doing.

"I've got one," she cried.

The young man was still face down under the seats. Bootsy was leaning down holding one foot in both hands. Noah felt trapped again. If Bootsy could be brave, he would have to be, too.

He sat down in back of her and felt around on the floor for the other leg. He was relieved that when he picked up the foot, the knee bent easily. Perhaps the young man didn't want to escape.

"Hang on, Bootsy!" he cried. "I've got it!"

By the time Adam and Mr. Warner were partway down the aisle, the picture ended and the lights came on.

Mr. Warner blew his whistle and hollered, "Quiet! Walk out slowly!"

Adam glanced back and saw two policemen helping the boys and girls leave the theater. He was afraid they would let the young man escape.

"We've got him!" yelled Noah.

Adam and Mr. Warner ran down the aisle.

"So you have." Mr. Warner was puffing. "Little

Noah and a girl have captured him! What's all this about a stolen ring?"

"I don't know about a ring," Bootsy said. She was still bent over, hanging on to a large foot. "But he was grabbing our feet!"

Mr. Warner called a policeman to come get the young man.

"Take him away," he said. "He was bothering my kids."

"I caught him, Adam!" Noah cried. "What do you think of that?"

"Thanks for the help, Noah," Bootsy said. "It was easier after you got the other foot."

"Good work, little lady." Mr. Warner patted her on the head. "Next time call me; I'll do the tackling!"

Bootsy tossed her pigtails and went to find her friends.

Mr. Warner took Noah and Adam into a little office to hear their story.

They told him about the popcorn boxes and the ring. They showed him the scratch on Noah's birthday watch. Mr. Warner just kept shaking his head.

"You've been watching too much TV," he said.

One of the policemen stuck his head in the door.

"That man looks like the one we're looking for," he said. "The one who stole the ring from the jewelry store. He was trying to hide in here."

"Well," Mr. Warner said, "we better get this thumb down to the police station."

Adam and Noah and Mr. Warner rode to the police station in a blue car. The driver let Noah ring the siren once. Adam worried some about how they would get the ring off his thumb.

At the police station, one of the policemen helped Adam wash his hands with lots of soap. Slowly, they were able to slide the ring off his thumb.

"I think these two boys will get a reward from the jeweler," the police chief said. "He'll be mighty pleased to get this ring back."

"Good," said Adam. "We'll buy a new glass for Noah's watch."

"Maybe we could get Bootsy a football helmet," Noah said. "After all, she helped."

4. Batty

Noah, sitting on the front steps of his house, decided that this was the hottest Saturday afternoon he had ever known. His swimming trunks under his jeans made him hotter still.

The tired cries of his baby brother came through the open window behind him. Bobby had been wailing all night, and their mother had been very cross this morning.

"Hurry up, Adam," muttered Noah, looking down the street. "Let's go swimming."

But only Helen or Ellen, whatever her name was, was coming down the street. She was carrying a small pink bundle.

"Taking your dolly for a walk?" jeered Noah.

Helen or Ellen tossed her head. "It's a cat," she said. "I just got it."

Noah got up and looked at the little head peering from the pink blanket. It had very big ears and a long pointed nose.

"That's a funny-looking cat," he said.

"It's a good cat," said Helen or Ellen. "It's young now. Maybe it will look better when it grows up."

"I don't think it will," said Noah. "Where did you get it?"

"Mary gave it to me. She lives way over at Sixty-third and Greene streets. We go to the same piano teacher," Helen or Ellen replied. "Her mother won't let her keep it because they live in an apartment."

"It has a funny-looking tail, too," Noah said, looking at the other end of the bundle. "What's the rest of it like?"

"You can see for yourself," the girl said. "Hold it for a minute."

Noah took the little bundle and pushed the blanket aside.

"Wow!" he said. "It's little. Are you sure it's a cat?" He looked up.

Helen or Ellen had moved away. "What else would it be?" she asked. She kept edging down the street.

"Wait!" Noah yelled. "Take your cat!"

The girl was moving fast now. She stopped and called over her shoulder, "My mother won't let me keep it, either. It's all yours, Noah!"

She turned and ran fast down the street and around the corner.

Noah didn't think that he could catch Helen or Ellen because her legs were longer than his and it would be hard to run holding the cat.

Bobby was still crying. Noah knew that this was not the time to argue with his mother about his keeping the cat. Anyway, the doctor had said no pets for Noah while Bobby was young. The hair made Bobby sneeze and cough. What could he do with a cat?

Noah was pleased to see Adam coming along.

"Hi, Adam!" he called. "I have something for you!"

Adam hurried along and looked down at the little animal.

"What is it?" he asked.

"It's a cat, a little one. I thought you'd like it," Noah said.

"No," said Adam. "I wouldn't. Anyway, my father doesn't like cats."

"They don't make him sneeze or anything, do they?" Noah asked.

"They don't have to," said Adam. "He just says, 'No cats.' Come on, let's go swimming."

"What will I do with it?" Noah was worried. "I can't keep it because of Bobby. Helen or Ellen just dumped it on me and ran."

"Don't you want to go swimming?" asked Adam.

"Of course I do! First I have to give the cat to someone. I can't just leave it here. It's too little."

"Maybe it isn't a cat," said Adam. "The tail doesn't look like a cat's; it's too bushy. Maybe it's a dog."

"Don't you want a dog, then?" Noah asked hopefully.

"Look here, Noah. I don't want it whatever it is. I want to go swimming."

Noah looked up and down the street. There were no kids in sight.

"Say," he said, "I bet all the kids are at the park. Let's go over there and I'll give it to somebody."

"That's four blocks in the wrong direction," Adam pointed out. "From there, it's ten blocks to the pool."

"Boy, that old water will feel even better when we get there." Noah wrapped up the little animal and started off. Adam followed rather slowly.

By the time they got to the park, Noah was tired. The little animal was light, but even so, carrying it made the four blocks seem very long. He sat down on the first shady bench to rest and put the pink bundle down beside him. Fortunately, the cat slept most of the time.

Adam wandered over to watch some boys with bats and a softball. The boys were a little older than Adam, and none of them looked as though he wanted a cat. Certainly not a funny-looking one.

A mother and a two-year-old girl walked by Noah's bench.

"Pussy, pussy," yelled the little girl, running toward the small head peeking out of the blanket.

Noah picked up the bundle just in time. He realized that he better hold it as long as the little girl was around.

"Mustn't touch pretty pussy," the mother said. She looked more closely. "It *is* a pussy cat, isn't it?"

"It's a cat," Noah said shortly.

"Will it scratch?" the mother asked, sitting down beside Noah.

"I think so," Noah said, glaring at the little girl. "I think it bites, too."

The little girl backed away and began to play with her ball.

"It's nice to see a boy taking such good care of a pet," the mother said.

Noah wondered about giving the cat to the woman. But with that little girl around all the time, the cat wouldn't stand a chance. The little girl picked up the ball and threw it hard — at Noah's head. He caught it in one hand and threw it as far as he could. The little girl ran after it.

The woman laughed. "Thanks for playing with Susy," she said. "She wears me out."

A woman pushing a baby carriage came along and sat on the other side of Noah. Noah felt uneasy between the two women and thought of joining Adam, but the boys had finally started a game. Adam seemed to be playing left field.

"Why, look at that," the second mother said to Noah. "You have a baby, too!"

"It's a cat," he pointed out. "A young cat."

"It doesn't look like most cats, does it? With those ears, it looks almost like a rabbit."

Noah looked uncertainly at the little face in his arms. He hadn't thought of a rabbit.

"No," he said. "Look at the tail!" He opened the bundle.

"My, yes, it's no rabbit!" the first mother exclaimed. "What a bushy tail for a cat!"

"More like a squirrel's," the second mother said thoughtfully.

The little animal woke up and yawned.

"It's rather a cute thing," the first mother said, "with that yellowish-brown color and the dark streak across its eyes and down its nose. Such a long nose!"

The cat started to squirm around and chew the blanket.

"Why, it's hungry!" cried the second mother.

"What do you feed it?" asked the first mother.

Noah started to squirm too. He hadn't thought of feeding it anything.

"Why, milk of course," said the second mother. "All babies drink milk, don't they?"

"Cats like milk," Noah said.

"Say, look." The second mother picked up a baby bottle from the carriage. "My baby is sound asleep and he left two ounces of milk. He never finishes his bottle. Do you want to give it some?"

"I don't have a dish," Noah said.

"I'll bet it will take a bottle," the first mother said. "Go ahead, try it. Come, Susy, sit on my lap and see the funny baby get its bottle."

Noah felt very foolish. He wished the women would go away. More than that, he wished he had never seen Helen or Ellen. The little animal wiggled and made funny noises. He guessed it was hungry.

He took the bottle and held it to the animal's mouth. It pushed the bottle away and chewed the blanket.

"Squeeze some milk out on the tip," the second mother said. "Then it will know what's in the bottle."

Noah shook the bottle until a couple of drops came out. This time the animal licked them off. Pretty soon it took the tip into its mouth and began to suck. Noah couldn't help feeling pleased. The women were delighted.

When the milk was almost gone, Noah looked up and saw Adam standing in front of the bench, staring at him. Without a word, Adam walked away. Noah could tell by the way he held his shoulders high that Adam was angry. He looked as though he would walk right out of the park. Noah felt a lot better when he saw Adam sit down under a tree a long way from the bench.

When the bottle was empty, he gave it back to the

woman with the baby. She laughed. "It's the kind you throw away," she said.

Noah got up, dumped the bottle into the trash can beside the bench, muttered "Thanks," and went after Adam.

Adam couldn't wait until Noah joined him.

"Do you know how you looked?" he demanded. "Sitting in a row with a bunch of mothers giving that thing a bottle? What if those boys had *seen* you?"

He rolled on the ground, groaning. "What if they thought *I* knew you? My friend, holding a batty cat in a pink blanket, giving it a bottle!" He rolled and groaned on the grass.

"I guess it did look funny," Noah said in a small voice.

"Look funny!" Adam groaned. "You looked like a little mother!"

"Well, the cat was hungry," Noah said. "And it likes this pink blanket even though it is hot."

"You just go on being a mother if you want to, but not around *me*," Adam said. "I'm going swimming." But he rolled over, face down on the grass.

Pretty soon Adam went on talking. "What an awful Saturday! It's hot, and we could be swimming instead of taking the baby to the park! Those big kids made me play left field and never hit one to me! I just chased the ball all the time, with them yelling at me."

Noah couldn't think of anything to say. He hadn't had a good Saturday, either.

The little animal seemed to feel better after the milk. It squirmed off Noah's lap and crept over toward Adam, who was still lying on the grass. It sniffed him, then began to lick his ear.

"Hello, Batty," Adam said, turning his head around. He began to rub the little animal under the chin. "You know, you wouldn't look so funny if you weren't supposed to look like a cat."

"Those mothers thought he was a squirrel or a rabbit," Noah said.

"Mothers don't know everything," Adam said. The little animal sat down and put its nose in the air. It liked being rubbed under its chin. "I'd like to know what he is if he isn't a cat," Adam said.

"Sure," said Noah. "Maybe if he's something else, someone would want him."

"Where did Helen or Ellen get him?" Adam asked.

"Some girl named Mary over on Sixty-third and Greene," Noah answered.

"If we could find her, I bet she'd know what Batty is," said Adam, "or tell us where she got him."

"There's a bus on Greene Street," Noah said. "Let's go. Please, Adam. You like to find out things!"

"I don't have any money. You don't need it for swimming," Adam said.

"I have some money," said Noah, jumping up. "I brought some to buy stuff to eat. You won't have to pay me back."

"I should hope not, Little Mother," said Adam.

Noah wrapped Batty in the pink blanket and they started for Greene Street, which ran along the other side of the park. They went the long way around, so as not to pass the mothers' bench or the baseball game.

When the bus came, it was crowded, and they had to sit on the back seat. Noah put the end of the blanket over Batty's head, but people still looked at him in some surprise.

It was very bumpy on the back seat, but it was good to sit down after all that walking.

The bus swayed along and jerked to a stop at every corner. The smell of gas came in the window on the hot breeze.

Batty gave a little jump, and sour milk shot out of his mouth onto Noah.

"Wow," said Adam. "It smells!"

The people in front of them turned around.

Batty gave another small jump.

"Let's get out!" said Noah. "He's going to do it again!"

They got out at the next corner.

"I hope he's not sick," said Noah.

"You smell awful," Adam complained.

"I should have put him over my shoulder and

patted him after the bottle," Noah said. "It was the bumps that did it."

"Shut up," Adam growled. He walked ahead of Noah.

The sign on the next corner said 43rd Street. The boys sat on a little wall.

"We can't walk twenty blocks," Adam said.

Noah looked at Batty. The cat seemed all right. He bounced the little animal up and down. No more milk came up.

"I think he's all right now," Noah said. "We can take the next bus."

Adam counted Noah's money. "If we do," he said, "we'll use up all the money. We can't walk home from there."

"Maybe Mary will lend us the money," Noah said.

"I bet she won't," said Adam.

Noah was silent. His face was red, he smelled awful, and it almost seemed that he was about to cry.

Adam felt mad at him, but he couldn't help feeling sorry for him, too.

"OK," he said, "we'll take the bus. But sit near the door and don't sit beside me. I guess we'll get home somehow."

The next bus was not crowded, and Noah sat by the door. Adam sat across from him and watched the street signs. They got off at 63rd Street.

The boys stood on the corner and looked down 63rd Street. Rows of large apartment houses lined the street.

"Wow!" said Adam. "How do you find anyone here? What's Mary's last name?"

Noah thought hard. He couldn't remember if Helen or Ellen had told him. He didn't want to tell Adam that.

Adam turned around and looked across 63rd Street.

"Look!" he yelled. "Look over there! The zoo!"

"Yes," said Noah. "The class went there once."

"The zoo! They know all about animals! They'll tell us about Batty!" cried Adam.

"I only remember elephants and lions in there," Noah said.

"Come on," said Adam. "We should have thought of the zoo before!"

They crossed the street and went to the gate. There was a sign on the gatehouse saying CHILDREN 50¢.

Noah was too tired to talk. He sat down on a bench beside the gatehouse, holding Batty in his lap. They both looked pretty sad.

Adam walked over to the ticket window.

"We have an animal here," he said. "We want to ask someone about him."

"Visitors aren't allowed to take animals into the zoo," the man said.

"We don't want to go in," Adam said. "Maybe

someone could just come and look at him through the fence?"

"Look, sonny," the man said, "the people who work here have plenty of animals to look at inside the fence."

Adam started to turn away. Then he thought of the wasted Saturday afternoon, the long walk home, and never knowing what Batty was.

"Please, sir," he said. "We've walked and walked. We've spent all our money on buses. We wanted to go swimming and it's very hot. Won't you please help us?"

The ticket man leaned out the window and peered at Noah on the bench.

"You do look all in," he agreed. "I'll call Dr. Foster. Dr. Foster never gets mad." He picked up the telephone.

Adam joined Noah on the bench and after a minute the man stuck his head out the little window.

"Dr. Foster will be right out." The man sounded surprised.

The boys watched the few people coming through the gate. They were mostly tired-looking mothers and children.

Suddenly, a large, gray-haired woman came through and hurried toward them. Her face lit up with a warm smile when she saw Batty.

"You wonderful boys!" she exclaimed. "You found him and brought him home!"

"Does he live here?" Noah asked in surprise.

"He certainly does. We've been looking for him since early this morning," she said.

"What is he?" Adam asked. "He's not a cat."

"He's a bat-eared African fox," Dr. Foster said. "He's a young cub, just three weeks old today."

She put out her arms to take Batty, but something about the way Noah was holding the little animal made her stop.

She really looked at the boys for the first time. They felt less tired when she smiled at them.

"Come along with me," she said. "I want to hear all about how you found him."

She waved at the ticket man, and the boys followed her through the gate into the zoo.

"A bat-eared fox!" said Noah. "We called him Batty because we thought he was a funny cat!"

"It's a good name for him anyway," Dr. Foster said.

They stopped to look at the elephants. One of them had a baby by her side.

"I'm glad I didn't have to carry one of those all afternoon," Noah said. "What if an elephant had spit up on me in the bus!"

Dr. Foster looked surprised. "You've been on a bus?" she asked. "We thought the cub — Batty — had gotten under the big fence around the zoo because the foxes' outside run is near it. We thought he would be nearby."

"Some girl gave him to me in front of my house," Noah explained. "I live in Kennyton."

"I know, I know!" Adam yelled so loud that several giraffes turned to look at him. "Mary lives over there on Greene Street. I bet she found him near your fence. Her mother wouldn't let her keep Batty, so she took him to her music lesson near where we live. She gave him to Helen or Ellen, and she dumped him on Noah!"

"My, what a big day you've had, Batty," Dr. Foster said. She looked worried. "I wonder how he feels?"

Noah pushed the blanket aside, and they all looked at the sleeping cub.

"Well," said Noah, "I think he's all right now. He spit up some milk on the bus but I think it was because the bus bounced so much, and he'd just had his bottle."

"Bottle?" Dr. Foster asked.

"A mother in the park let him finish her baby's bottle. It was a healthy-looking baby," said Noah. "Was that all right?"

"Well, I guess he was hungry," Dr. Foster said.

"Noah looked awful!" Adam shuddered. "Like Little Mother, sitting between two big ones with Batty wrapped up in that pink blanket having a bottle!"

"It wasn't my fault," Noah said. "Those mothers just about made me do it. Besides, Batty was hungry. You better stop calling me 'Little Mother.' "

For a moment Dr. Foster looked as though she might laugh, but she didn't.

"Noah is a good name for someone who takes care of animals," she said.

"Sure it is!" Noah said. "Why didn't I think of that?"

"Let's go this way and look at another kind of fox," Dr. Foster said.

They stopped in front of a big fenced pen with a family of red foxes in it.

"I'd know they were foxes anywhere," said Adam. "I should have guessed that Batty was one."

"Their ears are a lot smaller than the bat-eared fox," said Dr. Foster. "We see a lot of pictures of this kind of fox. Anyway, you wouldn't expect to see a fox in the city."

"Batty has a real fox tail," Noah pointed out. "It's kind of bushy and hangs down. A cat's tail sticks up."

"Come along," said Dr. Foster. "I want to look at Batty in my office and see if he's all right after his big day. Then he goes back to his mother."

"Oh, I'm glad he has a mother." Noah sighed.

"Me too!" said Adam.

They went into a building marked SMALL MAMMAL HOUSE. Just to the left of the door was Dr. Foster's office. It had a desk and a lot of books like any office, but it had a sink and a white table like a doctor's office.

The first thing Dr. Foster did was to wet a towel and wash off the sour milk from Noah's shirt.

"Thank you!" said Adam.

"I guess I'm used to it," Noah said. "I have a baby brother. I wish he'd sleep as much as Batty."

"African foxes are largely nocturnal animals," Dr. Foster said.

"That means they sleep in the day and are up at night," Adam said.

"My brother was nocturnal last night," Noah said. "My mother was cross this morning."

"It's not easy, being a mother," Dr. Foster said. "Or being a Noah either."

She asked Noah to put Batty on the table while she examined him. Noah kept patting his head so that he wouldn't be upset.

"Why does he like that dumb pink blanket?" Adam asked. "When it's so hot?"

"He doesn't mind the heat. It's hotter than this in Africa," Dr. Foster said. "Foxes dig burrows in the ground, so he likes to get under things."

"Why are his ears so big?" Noah asked.

"We think they help cool him," said Dr. Foster. "They act like little air conditioners. The blood in the blood vessels gets cooled by the air, and then cools the rest of the body as it passes through."

Dr. Foster finished examining the little fox. "He seems fine," she said. "Thanks to you two boys. I think he's a very lucky little fox to have met Adam and Noah."

"I'd have kept him," Noah said, "but the baby sneezes at pets."

"That wouldn't have worked," Dr. Foster explained. "No wild animal should be a pet. It's not right for the boy or the animal."

"We're glad to find out what he is," Adam said. "I never heard of a bat-eared fox before."

"You should come to the zoo more often," Dr. Foster said. She opened her desk and took out a little book. "Here's a book of tickets for the zoo so that you and Noah can come whenever you want."

"Wow, that's great," said Adam. "We won't have to pay to get in. We know how to get here on the bus now."

"We don't have any money left for the bus to get

home," Noah said. "We had to get off and then on again when Batty spit up. Can you lend us some money to get home?"

"I can do better than that," Dr. Foster said. "I'll drive you home. I'll be leaving at five; it's almost that now. Come along, we'll take Batty to his mother."

"Good," said Adam. "I wondered what a grown-up one looked like."

Dr. Foster carried Batty, and Noah took the blanket because he had gotten used to carrying it.

"We usually keep an animal away from the others for a while if he's been out with people," Dr. Foster said. "But the keeper says Batty's mother won't eat or feed her other cubs ever since Batty disappeared."

They went out of the office and through a door into a large room. On either side of a wide aisle were large cages for the small animals. Each cage had a small fenced yard at the back of it.

It was quiet and the light was dim. In the first cage was a sloth hanging upside down from a bar. In the next cage they saw a small sharp face and long ears turned toward them. The nose wiggled and twitched as they drew near.

Quietly, Dr. Foster opened a small door and put Batty inside. The mother fox made chucking noises, and Batty squeaked and whined. Soon the mother fox was licking her cub, and Batty was rolling around waving his legs with joy.

Noah gave a big sigh. "I'm glad she's a good mother," he said.

"I guess Batty's ears will get even bigger than they are now," Adam said, looking at the mother fox.

"Yes," Dr. Foster said. "A full-grown fox has ears four and a half inches long. They look even bigger on such a small animal. This fox is half as big as a red fox."

Two cubs who had been sleeping curled up in a corner came over to play with Batty.

"Batty doesn't look funny-looking anymore," Adam said.

"I guess we'd be funny-looking if someone thought we should look like a monkey," said Noah.

They watched the foxes until Dr. Foster said they would have to go.

"It's been a good Saturday, in a way," Noah said, as they were walking to the parking lot.

"It ended up good," Adam agreed. "Or it will." He stopped as they passed a trash can.

"Noah, put that pink blanket in there!" he ordered.

5. The Airport

The airport express bus stopped at the corner of Pine and 52nd Street, and Adam and Noah hopped on board.

"This trip is going to take all our money," Noah said. "Seventy-five cents one way; that's a dollar-fifty each. We won't be able to buy anything to eat."

"You wanted to go," Adam said. "We've saved up for this trip. It's going to be more fun than eating."

"I do want to see planes come zooming in to land," Noah said. He zoomed his left hand around and landed it on the back of the seat in front of them.

"I'd like that, too," said Adam. "But I want to find out just how you get a ticket and find the right plane to get on. I might want to do that someday."

"Where will you go?" Noah asked.

"I don't know yet," Adam answered. "I just want

to be ready to go if I get the chance. My uncle went to Chicago last month."

The bus made one more stop before it went to the airport. A well dressed young man got on and sat in front of the boys.

"You can tell he's going to fly somewhere," Noah said. "He's got a suitcase, a dark suit, and a white shirt. I wonder where he's going?"

The young man shifted in his seat and looked out the window.

"Let's find out!" said Adam. "Let's follow him until he gets on the plane, and we'll see just how you do it."

"I want to watch the planes come zooming in for a landing," Noah objected.

"When he gets on the plane, we'll go where we can watch his plane take off," said Adam. "It will almost be like we're going, too."

"OK," Noah agreed. "Afterward, we'll hang around and watch some land, too."

The airport was not busy this Saturday morning, and Noah and Adam had no trouble following the young man. Several times, Noah went in and out of the doors that open when one gets near them, but Adam kept his eye on the young man.

"Wow, look at all this carpet," said Noah, catching up with Adam. "There must be miles of red carpet in here. My mother would hate to have to clean up this place."

They crossed the red carpet to a high counter marked SKYHIGH AIRWAYS. They stood on either side of the young man as he talked to a woman standing behind the counter. The young man did not look at them.

"We — I want a ticket to New York," he said. "On the eleven-fifteen plane."

"Three tickets, sir?" the woman asked.

"No, one ticket," he snapped.

She pushed some buttons on a little machine and it clicked for a minute.

"We have a seat for you, sir. That will be eighty dollars." She began to write out his ticket.

The boys watched with great interest as the young man counted out the money. Adam whistled softly. He had never seen $80.00 all at once before.

"Here's your ticket, sir. Gate Six, Flight Five-sixty-five," she said. "Check in at the gate and get your boarding pass and seat number."

The man looked up at the big chalkboard behind the counter. Adam looked, too. On the left side was a list of numbers. Adam found 565 and, across from it, NY — On Time — Gate 6.

"Say, that's good," he said. "That board tells you where to get on the plane and that it will leave on time."

"It doesn't tell me," Noah said. "Look out! He's getting away from us."

The young man had moved fast. He was just

Skyhigh

rounding a corner. The boys ran after him and caught up with him going up some wide stairs. More red carpet covered these.

At the top of the stairs a sign reading GATE 6 pointed to the right. The young man looked at a big clock on the wall and went over to a newsstand beside a row of phone booths.

"The plane doesn't leave for half an hour," Adam said.

While the young man looked at the books and papers, the boys looked at the little planes, tiny parachutes, and pink stuffed bunnies on the counter.

"It's lucky we don't want any of that junk," Adam said. "Things cost a lot in an airport."

When the man had bought his paper he still did not go toward Gate 6. He went into a small lunchroom near the newsstand. He got a cup of coffee and sat down with his back to the boys.

Adam and Noah stood outside the lunchroom and looked through the window at the things on the counter just inside.

"That cherry pie looks good," Noah said. "But I think I'd like some of those cinnamon buns better."

"Don't!" said Adam.

"Look at those doughnuts!" Noah went on. "One doughnut wouldn't cost much."

"We have to save all our money to get home," Adam said.

Noah sighed. "It's all right for you; you're not

hungry. We passed some phone booths. Sometimes you find dimes in the pay phones."

"I'll watch our passenger and you look," Adam said.

Noah went back to the phone booths near the newsstand. There were six of them in a row. Five of them were empty. He slid a quick finger in each of the holes marked COIN RETURN, but there were no dimes. He glared at the lady in the last booth, but she kept on talking.

Just then the young man came by, walking fast, with Adam right behind him.

Noah caught up with them. "There must be a lot more phones in this place," he said. "I'll check them when our man takes off."

The gate was not a gate at all but a long wide hall with windows on both sides. The gate widened here and there into a large room with seats in it.

There was a knot of people standing part way down the hall. The young man squirmed his way into it.

"Let's go around the crowd," Adam said. "We don't want to lose him. We can pick him up on the other side."

They walked around the waiting group and found that everyone had been stopped by a barrier. "This is where passengers get searched," Adam said. "Let's watch here."

They sat down on a bench against the wall and

watched a woman in uniform run a machine that had a moving belt going through a little box with open ends.

Two women put their handbags on the belt, and the handbags were carried through the box.

"That's to see if there are any bombs in their bags," Adam explained.

Then the women, one at a time, walked through a doorway that stood alone, without any walls.

"That's to see if they have guns in their pockets," Noah said. "I've seen that on TV. A buzzer goes off if they do. I hope our guy is clean."

Next came a young woman in a smart blue uniform and a white cap with "Airport Aide" printed above the brim. There were three children following her; one was as big as Adam.

"I guess those kids are flying alone," Noah said. "She puts them on the right plane."

"We wouldn't need any help," Adam said. "We have it all figured out."

Finally, their young man walked through the doorway without setting off any buzzers. The boys thought of following him, but a guard looked at them as if he knew that they were not flying anywhere. They went back to their bench.

"Look," Noah said. "That first room has Flight Five-sixty-five beside it. I bet our man goes in there."

Sure enough, the young man turned into the

room, and as he did so the loudspeaker said, "Flight Five-sixty-five, now boarding."

The people in the room lined up and began to walk through a little door in the back of the room. A man stood there to make sure everyone had a boarding pass.

Adam stood up so that he could see better. The young man went to a desk in the room, and a man checked his ticket and gave him a strip of cardboard. The young man put his ticket in his pocket and, holding the boarding pass, went through the little door. The two boys jumped up. "Where can we see the planes take off?" Adam asked the guard.

"Go back to the newsstand and turn right. Go to the end and you'll find stairs up to the observation deck," he said.

The boys ran down the red carpet. Noah saw that the lady was still in the phone booth. They turned right and raced to the end of the building and up the stairs.

They found themselves on a long open deck. The wall around it was just the right height to lean on and look over at the planes below.

"There's good old Flight Five-sixty-five," Adam cried, pointing almost below them. "See our man at the end of the line?"

There were a few other people on the deck. Some of them were waving at the passengers going up the steps into the plane.

"Let's wave to our man," Noah said.

They yelled, "Goodbye" and "Have a good trip," and Adam even yelled, "Bon Voyage," but their man didn't seem to hear them. Finally, when he was on the top step, just before he went into the plane, he raised his hand to them. Two men then wheeled the steps away.

"That was nice of him," Noah said. "I don't think he liked us much."

"I'm sorry to see him go," Adam said. "We learned a lot from him. Airports are easy, once you know your way around."

"The eighty dollars isn't easy," Noah said.

It was warm and sunny on the deck, and the boys enjoyed watching three men who were finishing loading the plane. Suitcases were rolled out on carts and put in the back door of the plane.

"I hope his suitcase is there," Noah said. "It was a nice new one."

When the doors were closed, a man holding a white paddle in each hand walked in front of the plane and guided the pilot while he turned his plane slowly around. Then the plane rolled far out onto the runway.

"He's lucky to be really flying somewhere." Noah sighed.

The plane stopped a minute and they could hear the engines roar. Then it rolled faster and faster down the runway and rose into the air.

"Takeoff!" yelled Adam.

"Zoom, zoom, ZOOM!" cried Noah.

They stood for a minute, feeling a little sad. Then a plane landed on another runway and taxied slowly to where Flight 565 had been.

"Well," said Adam, "I guess we've done everything here."

"Everything but fly," said Noah. "I'm still hungry."

"I'm hungry, too," Adam said. "As well as thirsty. I guess we better go home."

They walked down the stairs and along the red carpet to the newsstand.

"It would have been good if we'd seen someone make the buzzer go off when they went through that horseshoe," Noah said. He saw that the sixth phone booth was empty now. He went in and felt the coin-return slot. It was empty.

As he turned to leave the booth, he stepped on something smooth and slippery. He shot out of the booth as if he were on one ski, and sat down hard at Adam's feet.

"Ouch!" he cried. "Was that a banana peel?"

"Wow, no," Adam said. "Look at this!"

A long brown-leather wallet lay open on the red carpet. Two airplane tickets and two boarding passes had fallen out of it.

Noah got up, and they both stared down at the wallet as the loudspeaker spoke above them.

"That's a man's wallet," Noah said. "The woman who was in the booth couldn't have lost it. Whose is it?"

Adam picked up the wallet and the tickets. "The tickets belong to Mr. and Mrs. Worthington," he said.

Noah picked up the boarding passes. "They say Flight Seven-o-eight, Gate Ten," he said.

"Last call for Flight Seven-o-eight," the loudspeaker said. "Last call for Flight Seven-o-eight."

"They won't be able to go without their tickets!" Adam cried.

"Quick!" cried Noah. "Let's find Gate Ten. We can catch them there!"

They had not passed any gates on their way to the observation deck, so they turned and raced down the red carpet in the other direction. Adam had pushed the tickets back into the wallet, and Noah held on hard to the boarding passes.

As they passed Gate 8 the loudspeaker said again, "Last call for Flight Seven-o-eight." It sounded as though it meant it this time.

When they got to Gate 10, they turned and ran down to another handbag machine and a doorway.

"I forgot about this," gasped Adam. "Do you think they'll let us through?"

The guard looked surprised, but seeing the boarding passes in Noah's hand, he waved him through. Noah walked through and the buzzer did not go off.

"Good boy," said the guard. "Left your cap pistol at home today."

Adam stepped through, and the buzzer sounded loudly in his ears.

"Honest, I don't have a cap pistol!" he said. "I lost it last year!"

"Come over here and empty out your pockets," the guard said.

Noah danced up and down as Adam pulled out a broken tape measure, a bunch of keys, and three bent nails.

"That will have done it," the guard finally said. "Try again."

This time when Adam stepped through the doorway the buzzer was silent.

The boys were off and running once more.

"Hey," yelled the guard. "You forgot your stuff."

Adam ran back and grabbed the wallet, which he'd put down so that he could empty his pockets. He left the rest.

They passed three rooms before they saw a sign for Flight 708. The man at the desk had gone, but the one at the little door was checking the boarding passes of a man and woman. He waved the couple along and started to close the door when the boys raced over to him.

"Are you two traveling alone?" he asked. "An airport aide is supposed to be with you."

"We don't need an airport aide," Adam said, panting. "We're not traveling alone. We're —"

"We're trying to catch Mr. and Mrs. Worthington," Noah gasped. "They —"

The man took the boarding passes out of Noah's hand. He glanced through the door at the stairs beyond. "A couple just went through here," he said. "I guess they are your friends."

The boys ran down the stairs and over to the plane. The couple ahead of them was disappearing inside. Two men in white stood ready to move the steps.

Adam had reached the top of the steps and Noah was halfway up when Noah stopped.

"Hey, Adam," he called. "How can the Worthingtons be on the plane when we have their boarding passes?"

Adam stopped and looked back. A young lady in a uniform reached out and pulled him aboard.

"Up you go, sonny," a man in white said. The steps jiggled. Noah went up.

The young woman smiled and took the boarding passes out of Noah's hand. "You just made it. Find your seats. We're taking off."

"But look here," said Adam. "You see, we're —"

The young woman looked at the boarding passes in surprise. "You're first class," she said.

"We're looking for Mr. and Mrs. Worthington," Adam cried.

"Not now," the young woman said. She pushed them back into the plane and into some seats. "Stay here. The captain has the seat-belt sign on." She still smiled, but her voice sounded like their teacher's at the end of a rainy day.

She leaned over and fastened Noah's seat belt. Adam watched and fixed his own.

The boys felt the plane begin to turn and then roll out to the runway. They were too surprised to talk. The plane gathered speed, faster and faster, until it lifted off the ground.

"Zoom, zoom," Noah whispered softly. The seat-belt sign went off.

Adam leaned over Noah and they looked out the window. The ground seemed to fall away from them.

"We'll have to tell that lady soon that we aren't

supposed to be here," Adam said. "If she'll ever listen to us."

"I wonder where Mr. and Mrs. Worthington are," Noah said.

"I guess it doesn't matter much now." Adam leaned back in his seat. "We're in trouble with everyone, I guess."

"I thought that you had this all figured out," Noah said. "How could the Worthingtons be on this plane if we had their boarding passes? Tell me that!"

"If you're so smart, why didn't you think of that before?" demanded Adam.

"I guess because we've been running ever since we found the wallet," Noah said. "It's not easy to think when you're running. What do you think they'll do to us? They can't put us off now."

"Not unless they have parachutes," replied Adam.

"That might be fun, too," Noah said. "Look, we might as well have fun now, as long as we can."

They began to look around them. There were not many other passengers. Adam leaned into the aisle and looked back.

"Say," he said, "way in the back of us there are a lot of seats close together, and they're all full."

"She said that we were first class," Noah pointed out. "Maybe that's second class."

"Sure," said Adam. "Only the best for us!"

They found some buttons that made the backs of the seats lean back.

"We could take a nap like this," Adam said. "If it's a long trip."

"I wonder where we're going," Noah said.

"I forgot, I can tell," Adam cried. He got the tickets out of the wallet. The tickets were hard to read but pretty soon he said, "We're going to Washington."

"That's a good place, I guess," said Noah. "But how do we get home again?"

Adam looked at the tickets some more. "This says that Mr. and Mrs. Worthington have tickets to come back again but not for three days."

"Three days!" cried Noah. "We have to be home for dinner tonight! We only have seventy-five cents apiece. We can't eat for three days on that!"

"Maybe we can't use these tickets anyway," Adam said. "Maybe we won't get home at all."

They were quiet for a long time.

Finally, the lady in the uniform hurried down the aisle. She had a name tag pinned to her shoulder.

Adam put out his hand and stopped her.

"Miss Tinker," he said, "we have a problem."

She looked at them closely. "First time you've flown?" she asked. "There's a paper bag in the pocket of the back of the seat in front of you." She hurried by.

The boys found the bags in the pockets in front of them.

"They look like lunch bags," Noah said. "But they're empty."

Adam studied the writing on the bags. "They're kind of for after lunch," he said. "If you eat lunch and you shouldn't have."

"You mean you're supposed to be sick in those things?" asked Noah. "Why would you be sick?"

The plane began to rock a little and the Fasten-Seat-Belt sign went on.

"Remember our trip in the Ark?" Adam said. "If you can get sick on a river, I guess you can on a plane."

"I can't," said Noah. "I'm empty. I just remembered how hungry I am."

"I'm still thirsty," said Adam. The wallet had slipped onto the floor, and the tickets were on Adam's lap. He leaned down and picked up the wallet to put the tickets back in it. "There's money in here, too," he said.

"How much money?" asked Noah.

Adam counted the money without taking it out of the wallet. The plane kept bouncing around and he kept losing his place. At last he whispered, "One thousand and two dollars."

"You're crazy," said Noah. "The wallet isn't that fat."

"I counted it twice," said Adam. "One thousand

and two dollars! There are a lot of hundred-dollar bills."

"I didn't know that there were any hundred-dollar bills," said Noah. "I can't believe you're holding one thousand and two dollars!"

"I can't believe that we are flying to Washington," Adam said.

Miss Tinker, pushing a cart, went by them toward the front of the plane.

"Did you see that?" Adam asked. "She had all kinds of things to drink on that cart!"

"I think I saw pretzels, too," said Noah. "Pretzels would help."

"Sure, they would. I think there was a bottle of my favorite soda, too." Adam said. "I wonder how much it costs on an airplane."

"It can't be more than seventy-five cents, and we have that," Noah said.

"Yes, but we have to keep our money. It would be awful if we ever did get back to our airport and couldn't take the bus home." Adam leaned out into the aisle. "She's stopping at each seat and asking if anyone wants a drink."

They both looked at the wallet on Adam's lap.

"Remember the jeweler gave us a reward for getting his old ring back?" Noah asked.

The plane began to jiggle and bounce a little, and the seat-belt sign went on again.

A loudspeaker began to talk above their heads.

"This is Captain James speaking. I'm sorry that we are in a bit of rough air. I hope it won't last long. Please stay in your seats and keep your seat belts fastened."

"He sounds worried," Adam said uneasily.

"You think Mr. Worthington might give us two dollars for finding his wallet?" Noah asked. "Two dollars isn't much of a reward."

"I've been thinking about it," Adam said. "He might give it to us if he were here, but he isn't here."

Miss Tinker was handing out drinks to the people two rows in front of the boys.

"If he hadn't lost that old wallet we wouldn't be in this trouble," Noah pointed out. "It's his fault, in a way."

The plane suddenly dropped as though it were a fast elevator. Adam and Noah hung on to each other, and Miss Tinker smiled harder and clung to the cart.

When the plane steadied again, Adam said in a shaky voice, "We won't take the two dollars."

"Of course we won't," said Noah. "That would be stealing!"

Miss Tinker was still smiling when she stopped her cart beside them.

"Sodas for you two boys," she said, filling two glasses with ice and opening two bottles.

Adam shook his head no. His mouth was so dry at the sight of something to drink at last that his voice was more of a croak. "We haven't the money," he said.

Miss Tinker pulled down the little trays on the seat backs in front of the boys and put glasses and sodas and pretzels on them.

"You don't need money," she said. "These are on Captain James."

Adam drank half his soda in one gulp. "Ah — ah — " he said. "I'm glad we didn't use Mr. Worthington's money."

"It was that awful way the plane dropped that made us not do it," Noah said.

"I think we better make Miss Tinker listen to us," Adam said. "The plane might do it again."

"Sure," said Noah. "But first let's finish the sodas. Captain James might not want us to have them if he knew we weren't supposed to be here."

When they had finished, Adam found a button to push that made a light go on to call Miss Tinker.

The smiling Miss Tinker came and sat on the arm of Adam's seat.

"Now," she said, "what's your problem?"

"We are not Mr. and Mrs. Worthington," Adam said, handing her the tickets.

Miss Tinker finally stopped smiling as she read the tickets. "You certainly aren't," she said. "Tell me what happened."

Noah began when he slipped on the wallet while he was looking for dimes in the phone booth. He told about their race for Gate 10 and how Adam had set off the buzzer. Miss Tinker stopped him when he came to the door in the waiting room that led down the stairs onto the airfield.

"Wasn't there a man to check your passes before you went through the door?" she asked.

They told her what had happened.

"We tried to tell you when we got on the plane," Adam said, "but you didn't listen. You just made us sit down."

"Yes," Miss Tinker said. "The captain had signaled for takeoff."

"We tried to tell you again," Noah put in, "but you thought we were seasick. We weren't at all."

"Well, that's one good thing," Miss Tinker said. "I don't think anything like this has ever happened before. I'll have to get the captain."

She walked toward the front of the plane.

"I thought I'd feel better after we told her," Adam said. "But I feel worse."

"It's not so hard to explain to a lady who smiles all the time," Noah said. "I didn't think we'd have to tell the captain."

"Captains on ships can do anything. I read about them once," Adam said. "They can marry people or shoot people or anything they want."

"He can't marry us," Noah said reasonably. "He wouldn't shoot us here; it would scare the other passengers."

"I almost wish that you hadn't found this wallet," Adam said.

"I don't wish that yet," said Noah. "I'll wait and see."

Noah looked out the windows at the white puffy clouds. They looked soft and cottony and as though they might be fun to roll in.

Adam kept leaning out into the aisle to see if the captain was coming. It seemed a very long time before the door at the end of the first-class cabin opened.

Adam punched Noah in the ribs. "He's coming," he said, hardly moving his lips.

Captain James was a very big man. His uniform shone with silver buttons and wings, and his cap was pulled a little over one eye. His face was handsome, but he wasn't smiling as he walked slowly down the aisle, looking carefully at the passengers on either side. When he got to Adam and Noah, he stopped.

"Mr. and Mrs. Worthington?" he asked.

Adam sighed. "Yes," he said. "That's us."

Captain James sat on the arm of the empty seat in front of Adam and leaned over the back of it. He pushed his hat back a little and looked at each boy.

"Miss Tinker told me about your finding the wallet and the tickets," he said. "You were pretty smart to figure out where the plane was."

"That was because of Adam," Noah explained. "He wanted to find out just how you bought a ticket and how you could tell which plane to get on. So we followed a man and saw him get a ticket and boarding pass."

"The boarding pass tells you the flight number and the gate," Adam said.

"So it does," said the captain. His mouth was not smiling, but Adam thought maybe his eyes were. It made him feel a little better.

"If you were smart enough to figure out all that," the captain went on, "why did you think the Worthingtons were on the plane when you had their tickets and boarding passes?"

"I saw that we were wrong about that," Noah said. "But Miss Tinker had already pulled Adam aboard, and the men were jiggling the steps. It was too late to stop."

"It was late, all right," the captain agreed. He looked at the boys thoughtfully for a time while they admired the silver wings on his shoulder.

"Miss Tinker didn't let us explain," Adam said finally. "She grabbed our boarding passes and made us sit down."

"Miss Tinker is a quick one," the captain agreed again.

"The man at the door wouldn't let us explain either," said Noah.

"Most grownups don't let you explain things," Adam said. "Say, I bet he thought we were traveling with the Worthingtons!"

"Perhaps you've been in too much of a hurry to explain things right," the captain said. "Was there any money in the wallet?"

"Wow! Was there!" Adam said, handing the wallet to the captain. "One thousand and two dollars! I counted it twice."

The captain counted the money and whistled.

"I'd better get on the radio and talk to the airport," he said. "I'll bet Mr. Worthington has been worried sick."

"We're worried, too," said Noah. "How can we get home? We only have seventy-five cents each!"

"We'll settle you later," the captain said. "I'll be back." He hurried up the aisle.

"He was nice," Noah said. "We should have thanked him for the sodas."

"We can later," Adam said. "I wonder how you go about being a pilot?"

"Those were nice silver wings," Noah said.

When the captain didn't come back right away, the boys began to worry again.

"He wasn't mad," said Adam, "but he asked a lot of questions."

"I wonder what he meant by settling us?" Noah couldn't get interested in the clouds again.

When the captain came down the aisle again, he was smiling all the way.

"I talked to Mr. Worthington," he said, sitting down once more. "He's taking the next plane to Washington, and I'll leave the wallet at our desk there. He said he had been in a phone booth near the newsstand, and his wallet did have one thousand and two dollars in it."

"Of course it did," said Adam. "We didn't take any."

"We thought of borrowing some," Noah said, "but we decided not to. We decided not to before we found out that we didn't have to pay for the sodas."

"Thank you for the sodas," Adam said. "We were very thirsty."

"Oh, I don't pay for them," the captain said. "Skyhigh Airways does. Miss Tinker just says that.

I'm glad you didn't take any of Mr. Worthington's money, but I'm glad you thought of doing it."

"You are?" asked Adam. "We felt guilty just thinking about it."

"Sure," the captain said. "You wanted to, but you didn't. You felt too guilty. That's good."

"I guess you're right," Adam said. "I didn't think of that."

"The plane made that awful drop," Noah said. "That made us change our minds."

Captain James laughed. "That was a bad air pocket," he said. "It scared you into feeling even more guilty. The air pocket didn't make you not take the money; feeling guilty did."

"I never thought that feeling guilty was good," Adam said.

"Sure it is," the captain said. "It keeps us all out of a lot of trouble."

"I don't feel guilty about getting dimes out of pay phones," Noah said.

"Well, I guess that's different," Captain James agreed. "Now here's what Skyhigh Airways is going to do for you. We're proud to have such honest passengers, so we'll fly you back from Washington for free. You'll have almost an hour to wait in the airport, but you'll be home by five o'clock."

"That's great!" Adam cried. "We'll have another trip when we're not worried!"

"Noah can check the Washington phones for

dimes," the captain said. "If he doesn't find any, do you have enough money to get home from the airport?"

"Sure," said Adam. "We've saved our bus fare."

"Good," the captain said. "I've asked Miss Tinker to bring your lunch right away. That's free, too. Then she'll bring you up front and I'll show you how to fly this plane."

"Steak, french fries, and chocolate cake!" cried Noah when he saw the lunch trays.

"Wow!" said Adam. "I'm always going to fly with Skyhigh Airways!"

6. TV

Adam and Noah started along a path that led across a corner of the park. They were taking a short cut to City Avenue and 60th Street.

"It's a waste of a good Saturday," Adam said. "Going to some dumb kids' TV show."

"The tickets are free," Noah said.

"No wonder they're free," Adam said crossly. "They need a bunch of noisy kids in the studio to make the kids at home think they're having fun."

"There's a clown in the 'Saturday Fun Time Show,' and a dog that does tricks," Noah said.

"A poodle." Adam jeered. "A sissy little poodle!"

"I bet you don't want to go because the janitor at Channel Seven gave me the tickets, not you!" said Noah.

"Now that's a stupid thing to say," Adam said. "Really stupid."

The boys walked very slowly and didn't say anything for a while.

"I wanted to do something really special today," Adam went on. "Not just sit and watch a clown!"

"We've never watched them make a TV show," Noah pointed out.

"They just make a bunch of kids sit there and tell them when to clap and laugh," complained Adam. "Just like school, except there they tell you not to clap and laugh!"

"OK, OK." Noah stopped. "We won't go. What will we do?"

Adam stopped, too. "There isn't a good movie around."

"That's good," said Noah. "We don't have any money. Not even for food."

"Gangway for the TV crew!" A yell came from behind them.

Adam and Noah turned quickly. A bicycle with two boys on it came racing down the path heading right at them.

"Channel Seven is first with big park crash!" one of the riders sang out.

Adam and Noah stood together until the bicycle was almost upon them, and then they sprang apart and the bike shot between them.

"Your favorite announcer, Butch Gordon, will be right back," yelled the boy who was pedaling. The bicycle turned in a wide circle.

"Wow!" said Adam. "They almost got us!"

"Fresh kids!" said Noah. "I've seen them before."

"Sure," Adam said. "Butch Gordon is in the grade ahead of us in school. He looks different because he has a suit on!"

"That's right," said Noah. "The one in back is Lee something. He has a suit on, too, and a haircut."

"Something funny is going on," Adam said. "Why would they be dressed up on Saturday?"

"They're playing TV," said Noah thoughtfully. "I wonder if they know something we don't."

"They're circling back," Adam said. "If they try that again, we won't move. They'll have to turn away or else take a spill."

The boys walked faster but kept watching the bike as it swung around in a big circle. In a few minutes, it came tearing down the path in back of them again.

"Keep tuned, folks! Watch your screen as Channel Seven strikes again!" Butch called.

Adam put a firm hand on Noah's shoulder as the bike raced toward them. "We're not moving!" he yelled. Noah closed his eyes.

The bike tore at them but at the last moment swerved away. It tipped and wobbled as the boys aboard hollered. Finally, it righted itself and sped away.

"Well," said Adam. "We won that one."

"Just," said Noah. "We just won. They must be going to the kids' show at Channel Seven. But why would they be dressed up?"

"They're nuts," said Adam. "Trying to be tough like that and getting all dressed up to just sit in the crowd and clap."

They walked faster and came to City Avenue. They turned left onto the wide sidewalk and started down a gentle hill. A low wall separated the park from the sidewalk, and dry leaves from the park trees had piled up along it. Noah walked in them, scuffing them in front of him.

"There they are," said Adam. "Ahead of us. They're going to the TV station, all right."

"Sure they are," said Noah. "There's nothing else to do today. I'm glad they're ahead of us."

"They're still cowboying," Adam said. "Wow! Look at that!"

The bicycle swerved out to the curb and back to the walk. Then it made a tight figure eight and almost fell over.

"It looks like fun," Noah said. "I wish we had a bike. It would save a lot of money on bus fare."

"It would save us money after we had one," Adam agreed. "But it would cost a lot to buy one."

"That's a pretty old beat-up bike," said Noah.

"Look at that!"

The bike zoomed ahead with both boys' arms outstretched. They were making airplane noises.

"I think even an old beat-up bike would cost twenty dollars," Adam said.

As the boys watched, the front wheel of the speeding bike banged into the wall. They saw Butch's hands come down to grab the handlebars, but too late. The bike crashed into the wall, and the front wheel bounced over it. Lee flew off the back, and Butch and the bike fell in a twisted heap.

Adam and Noah stopped and waited. Nothing moved in the wreckage ahead of them.

"They must be hurt," Adam said slowly. "I mean really hurt."

The boys ran toward the wreck. Even as he ran, Adam had the feeling that he wanted to run the other way. He didn't like blood; he had fainted once when he cut his finger.

There was blood, all right. Lee's head had hit the stone wall when he flew off the bike, and blood streamed over his face. Blood and tears.

Noah knelt down beside him. He didn't have a handkerchief but a clean one was sticking out of Lee's suit pocket. He took it and wiped Lee's face.

Butch lay on his back. His face looked awful and he was biting his lips.

"It's my leg," he whispered to Adam.

Adam looked down and saw that Butch's leg seemed to be turned the wrong way.

"I'll get the bike off you," he said. He very carefully lifted away what was left of it, trying not to look at the crooked leg.

Adam looked up and down the street. There was no one walking on either sidewalk, and traffic was light on Saturday morning. He stood at the curb and waved at the first car that came along. It stopped, and a man came over to the boys.

"You have a busted leg, son," he said to Butch. "But the doctors can fix that. My son had a busted leg once, and he's on the high school football team now."

He took his own clean handkerchief and folded it up and showed Noah how to press it on Lee's cut. "The doctor can sew that up good as new," he told Lee.

"We need an ambulance," he said to Adam. "We can't move a broken leg."

"I'll call the police," Adam said. "We passed a phone booth at the corner. I'll run down there."

"Don't leave me," Butch said in a small voice.

"Right," said the man. "You stay here. I'll drive down and phone. I'll tell them to hurry."

Adam sat down beside Butch. Butch didn't look tough at all now. It was funny that he wanted Adam to stay with him, when just a little while ago he had been trying to run him down.

"I don't like cops," Butch said in a shaky voice. "They're always chasing me when I play ball in the street."

"They'll be nice to you now that you have a broken leg," Adam said.

He wanted to ask Butch if he really had been going to the TV studio and why he was all dressed up, but Butch was making faces and Adam knew that he was trying not to cry. Adam looked up and down the street again and whistled softly.

"Say," he said. "You're a good bike rider. I never saw anyone better. It was the stupid old bike that threw you. The front wheel came off. No one can ride a bike with the front wheel off!"

"Listen!" yelled Noah. "A siren!"

Adam went to the curb and waved to the ambulance. The two policemen looked very large and were very gentle. Adam told them about the accident, and while he was talking they put Butch on a stretcher and carefully slid it into the ambulance. They even put the bike in when Butch asked them to.

One of the policemen told Noah that he had done the right thing by pressing the cut on Lee's head. He got a clean pad out of the first-aid kit and sat in back so that he could keep on pressing.

"Will they be all right?" Noah asked anxiously.

"Sure they will, and we'll call their parents as soon as we get to the hospital," the driver said.

Adam and Noah watched the ambulance drive off.

"We'll be more careful when we get our bike," Noah said. "I won't try all that trick stuff when I'm near a wall."

"I'm bigger, so I'll probably pedal and steer while you hang on the back," Adam said.

"You think you'll be up front all the time?" demanded Noah. "What difference does it make who's bigger? My feet can reach the pedals just as well as yours!"

"No use arguing," Adam pointed out, "until we get our bike. Did you ask Lee why they were all dressed up?"

"No," said Noah. "I forgot all about it and the TV show, too. I'm glad I learned about pressing on a cut. Wow! The way the blood poured out of it before I —"

"Stop it." Adam shuddered. "They're gone now. Let's forget about them!"

"I might be a doctor," Noah went on. "It must be interesting to sew up a cut."

"Look at your watch," Adam said sternly. "Is it too late for that TV show?"

Noah pushed back his sleeve. "The show begins at eleven-thirty, but you have to be there pretty early to get in. It's after eleven now, but we might as well try. We're álmost there."

The next street was 60th, and they crossed it and then crossed City Avenue. On the corner was TV Station WHTT.

It was a large white building set in a green lawn. They walked up the driveway and on their right they saw a door marked STUDIO I, with a small group of kids in front of it. As they drew near, they could tell at once that they were too late. About a dozen girls and boys hung around the door or sat on the steps in front of it.

"You're too late," a girl said. "About a hundred kids were here pushing and shoving. We were here before a lot of them but we didn't have a chance!"

Adam and Noah sat down on the bottom step, a little way from the others. Their walk and the excitement of the accident had made them pretty tired. They just sat there, while Noah thought about being a doctor and Adam thought about how they were wasting a Saturday.

The door in back of them opened and a few hopeful kids moved toward it. A short man hurried out, and a guard inside banged the door closed again.

The short man was upset. He paced up and down in front of Adam and Noah, tugging at his tie with one hand and running the other hand over his bald head.

A tall young woman trotting around the outside of the building came over to him, her tight short curls dancing on her head.

"I'm ruined, Edna," the man said in a hoarse voice. "Ruined. Bob will have my head for this. He'll take it right off; you know he will! Those kids were to be here at eleven o'clock to rehearse with him!"

"I've been all over inside and out looking for those two," Edna said. "You checked in there?" She pointed to Studio I.

"I got that clown to call for them just before his show started. No luck. His show is *on now*, Edna. That means Bob Hunter's show is on in half an hour! And no kids! Bob will kill me. You know how he is, Edna. Then he'll fire me, and my wife — " Harry rubbed his head with both hands.

"Stop it, Harry. We have to think of something." Edna glanced at the few kids still on the steps. "I checked these leftovers a little while ago. Listen, boys," she called out. "Have any of you seen Harold Gordon and Arnold Leland?"

No one answered, and Harry and Edna hurried down the path, Harry yanking at his tie.

"Harold Gordon," Adam said slowly. "You don't think Butch —"

"Sure," said Noah, jumping up. "Butch's first name must be Harold!"

"And Lee's name is Arnold Leland," cried Adam, leaping to his feet. "We better tell Harry what happened to them!"

"Hey, Harry, wait!" they called as they ran down the path.

"We know where those boys are," Adam said when they had caught up to Edna and Harry. "They're in the hospital!"

"I knew it, I knew it," Harry moaned.

"What happened?" Edna asked.

"They fell off their bike," Noah said. "Lee had a terrible cut on his head. The blood was pouring down his face —"

"Butch Gordon had a broken leg," put in Adam.

"How could they do this to me?" Harry almost jerked his tie off. "Stupid kids can't even ride a bike!"

"They aren't stupid," Adam objected. "The front wheel hit the wall and came off."

"Why didn't someone tell me?" Harry asked.

"It just happened on their way here," Adam said. "We waited for the police ambulance to come. That's why we missed 'Saturday Fun Time.' "

"You'd think that two kids who were going to be on the 'Bob Hunter Show' might make an effort not to get half-killed —"

"Keep quiet, Harry," Edna said. "I have an idea."

"I have an idea too, Edna," Harry exclaimed. "*You* tell Bob that he won't have anyone to interview. We promised him two kids!"

"Shut up, Harry," Edna said. "Let's put these two boys on the show instead."

"That's crazy, Edna. Gordon and Leland went to Camp Tepee Town this summer. They were supposed to tell Bob how great it was for poor kids to get out of the hot city for two weeks."

"We're not poor," Adam said. "My dad just got a raise."

"Bob has all the notes on the camp. *He* could tell *them* about it," Edna said.

"I like the city," Noah said.

Harry looked at his watch. "No time to rehearse them."

"Don't you see?" Edna went on, "If *he* told *them* all about the camp and how maybe they could go *next* year, the boys would just have to say yes or no."

"No," Adam said.

Harry looked at his watch again and groaned. Then he really looked at the boys for the first time. He looked very doubtful.

Adam remembered Butch's and Lee's suits. He and Noah weren't dressed up at all. As a matter of fact, they were rather dirty from sitting on the sidewalk.

"You don't want us," he said, edging away. "We don't have our suits on and —"

Suddenly Harry's face broke into a wide smile.

"Perfect!" he said. "They're perfect, Edna! Bob will really go for these kids!"

"I don't think he will," said Noah. "And I don't want to go to camp." He edged away, too.

Harry quickly put a friendly hand on each boy's shoulder. "Not want to go to Camp Tepee Town?" he said in surprise. "They must be kidding, Edna. Everyone wants to get out of the city in the summer!"

"We like it here." Noah tried to pull away.

Edna put her arm through Noah's. "Do you realize you'll be on TV?" she asked. "Think of all the boys who would love that! I'll bet you never thought it would happen to you."

"Well," Noah said, "if I get to be a famous doctor it might happen."

Adam looked around to see if there were any boys nearby who wanted to be on TV, but all the kids had drifted off.

The boys were hustled into the main entrance of Station WHTT before they realized what was happening. Inside they were hurried down a hall to the right and stopped in front of a door that had BOB HUNTER printed on it.

"You just go in there and tell Bob there's no other way," Edna said. "What can he do?"

"I'm afraid to find out," Harry said.

Harry looked at his watch again and jerked his tie. "Twelve minutes to show time," he said.

"I know you can do it, Harry," Edna said.

Harry squared his shoulders and opened the door a little way.

"Is that you, Harry?" an angry voice bellowed from inside the room. "Where in the devil are those —"

Harry glanced back at Adam and Noah. They were drifting back down the hall. He pulled the door closed and whispered, "Ten dollars!" Then he opened the door again and strode in quickly.

The boys stopped.

"Ten dollars!" Adam said. "That's good money."

"I'm hungry, and I don't think my mother would want me to be on TV," Noah said uneasily.

"Quick, your names and phone numbers!" Edna cried. "I forgot that we must ask your parents."

When they had given their phone numbers to her, she began dialing a phone that hung on the wall a little beyond Bob Hunter's door. She glanced over her shoulder as she waited.

"We'll give you lunch in our cafeteria after the show," she called. "All you can eat."

"What do you think about all this?" Noah asked Adam.

"The trouble is, I haven't had time to think. Those two talk too fast," Adam complained.

"Yeah," Noah agreed. "And they push you around. Bob Hunter sounded even worse. He sure was mad at Harry."

"I wouldn't mind if he did take Harry's head off," Adam said. "I don't much like Harry."

"We could run for it right now," Noah suggested.

"Still, there is that ten dollars," Adam said.

"And a lot of lunch." Noah sighed. "I like a cafeteria because you can see what you're getting."

Edna turned from the phone. "Your parents say it is all right," she said. "They'll be watching. Your father said you forgot to put the trash out, Adam."

Just then a smiling Harry pulled open the office

door, and there was Bob Hunter, a big handsome man who looked very friendly indeed. Smiling and chuckling, he walked over to the boys and put an arm around each of them and gave them a hug.

"So you want to be on TV, do you?" he asked, but he didn't want an answer. He kept right on talking and walking the three of them down the hall.

"Here's what we'll do on the show," he said. "I'll tell you about Camp Tepee Town and you look at me and listen. I'll tell you that there's a lake, and you can ask, 'How big is the lake?' " He squeezed Adam's shoulder. "Get it? Sure you do! Then I'll tell you that there are animals in the woods, and you" — he squeezed Noah — "ask, 'What animals are there in the woods?' You can do that, can't you?"

There was a lot more, but Adam and Noah gave up listening. Ever since they had met Edna and Harry, people had been talking to them too fast. Bob's words buzzed around their heads like a bunch of flies.

Harry ran ahead of them and opened a door marked STUDIO II. "Good luck, Bob," he said.

"Good luck to *you*, Harry," Bob said. "You need it."

Studio II was a small, brightly lit room. There was a table with three chairs around it. Bob sat on one side of it and put Noah beside him and Adam at the end.

Adam and Noah looked at the large camera a few feet away from them and at the man standing beside it and another man beside him.

"Our cameraman, John, and our director, Art," Bob said.

"You're late," Art said. "Three minutes to go."

"Harry lost the real boys," Bob snapped. "We haven't rehearsed. I'll have to wing it."

Art shook his head and groaned. "Remember," he said to the boys. "Don't look at the camera!"

Art held up five fingers in front of Bob. He had a stopwatch in his other hand and jerked his finger down to show each second going by. It was very quiet in the room. Bob got his smile ready, and as the last finger fell he spoke into the camera.

"Good morning. This is the Bob Hunter Show. We have a treat for you today. You'll meet two fine young city boys who are interested in going to Camp Tepee Town next summer. They are — they are — " He ruffled his notes. "Let's let them tell us who they are." He looked at the boys.

Adam and Noah were so used to no one wanting them to answer that they didn't say anything.

"What's your name?" Bob smiled hard at Noah.

"Noah Carter," Noah said and kicked Adam under the table.

"Adam Tyler," Adam said, looking into the camera.

Bob Hunter talked on and on about Camp Tepee

Town and how good it was for boys to get out of the city, where there was nothing for them to do.

Noah discovered a silent TV screen high on the wall in back of the camera. There was Bob, all right, talking away on it, and there was Adam staring into the camera. The little guy between them didn't look much like himself.

He sat up taller and pulled his right ear. Sure enough, the boy on the screen pulled his ear. Noah pulled his other ear. It was a funny feeling to be making that small figure up there on the screen do whatever he did.

Adam went right on looking at the camera. He didn't want to particularly, but somehow he couldn't stop. Art, standing beside the camera, began making faces at him and jerking his thumb toward Bob. Adam watched him closely.

Noah saw that the camera had swung around and only Bob showed up there on the screen. He began to watch Art, too. Art pointed right at Adam and then put both hands around his own neck and pretended to choke himself.

"Adam," Bob said sharply, "Camp Tepee Town is on a lake. Do you want to know how big the lake is?"

Adam turned his head a little toward Bob but his eyes slid back to the camera.

"No," he said. "We swim in the city pools."

Bob tried to chuckle, but it didn't sound right.

"There are other things to do on a lake. Noah, do you know what they are?"

"We went on the river in a rowboat," Noah said. "It leaked, and I almost drowned."

"Well, well, that's too bad," Bob said, but he didn't sound very sorry. "Noah made a good point there, folks. Every boy learns to swim at Camp Tepee."

Noah started to say that he had learned to swim at the "Y," but Bob said that there would be a commercial break.

Soap powder appeared on the small screen.

"I'll get Harry for this; see if I don't," Bob said grimly. "He must have really tried to get kids like these two!"

"Look, kid," Art said fiercely to Adam. "Stop looking at the camera or I'll —"

"You stop making faces at him!" Noah said. "It's all your fault!"

Art leaned across the table and began whispering to Bob.

"I saw us on that little screen up there," Noah said to Adam in a low voice. "We did look pretty dumb."

"I don't want to look at the camera," Adam said. "I can't help it. I don't hear what Bob's saying. I hear him talking, all right, but not what he's saying."

"I bet Mother got all the neighbors to watch us," Noah said. "We look awful."

"My father is watching, too," Adam said. "He's a little mad already about my not putting the trash out."

"I guess they'll turn the camera away from us from now on," Noah said, "and no one will see us at all. They did that when I was pulling my ears."

"We can still talk," Adam said.

"I can't remember what he wants us to say," Noah said.

"That's the trouble!" Adam exclaimed. "We're on a talk show and they won't let us talk about what we want to talk about. They should let guests talk about what they want to."

"How can we do that?" asked Noah.

"We'll just have to jump in and try. I think that's what Bob means by 'wing it': just talk when you don't know what you're going to say."

"We can do that," Noah said.

"Sure," said Adam. "I won't look at the camera, and you leave your ears alone. Any chance we get, we'll speak up."

The commercials were over, and the camera was just on Bob.

"The boys learn about nature, too, at Camp Tepee Town," Bob said, looking up from his notes. "There are deer in the woods, and last summer the boys saw a fox and her cubs."

"That's interesting about foxes," Adam said. "I like foxes."

"Were they gray or red foxes?" Noah asked.

Bob looked surprised. He looked at his notes. "I'm not sure," he said.

"They must have been red ones," Adam said. "Dr. Foster at the zoo said they were the only ones in our state."

Noah saw that he and Adam were now on the screen. Adam wasn't staring at the camera and he didn't look dumb at all.

"I like African bat-eared foxes best," said Noah. "Dr. Foster told us all about them."

"Dr. Foster. Who is he?" Bob sounded uncertain, and he glanced at Art.

"Dr. Foster is a woman." Adam looked right at Bob. "She's in charge of the mammals at the zoo, and she knows everything about them. She's a good friend of ours."

"She is?" Bob asked in surprise.

"You see, we rescued Batty," Noah began. "Some girl — "

"Batty is a bat-eared African fox cub, and he got under the fence at the zoo," Adam interrupted. "We took him back, and now we go to see Dr. Foster all the time."

"Well, that's interesting," Bob said. "Does she—"

Art waved at Bob and pointed to his notes. Only Bob appeared on the screen now.

"Yes, indeed," he said. "Our guests have proved that boys are interested in animals. One more reason for you to send in your money so that city boys can go to Camp Tepee Town next summer. Another reason —" He began flipping over the pages of his notes.

"Some kids collect different kinds of rocks," Adam said.

"Of course they do." Bob seemed relieved. "I'll bet a lot of boys get interested in geology at camp."

"We've seen a lot of rocks at the Natural History Museum," Noah said. "There's a small room that's dark until you push a button, and then the rocks glow in different colors. Dr. Richards — he's the director — told us all about them."

"You know Dr. Richards, too?" Bob asked. "I heard him give a lecture once."

"Oh, yes," Adam said. "He likes us to tell him when we're in the museum."

"He does?" Bob seemed to have forgotten his notes. "Why?"

"Well, once I dropped my little dinosaur and it got kicked into the big scene with the bear and the snake," Noah said.

"I know that one," Bob said.

"We got inside to get Noah's dinosaur," Adam said. "And, well, the bear fell over and we met the director that way."

"How did you get in?" Bob leaned forward.

"There's a door —" Noah began.

"I don't think Dr. Richards would want us to tell

our viewers about that," Adam said quickly. "Even if it is locked now."

Bob grinned. "I guess you're right, Adam. I always wondered what it would be like inside one of those animal windows."

"Scary," Adam said. "It's too real but it isn't real."

Art had been waving at Bob, and now he signaled for a commercial.

A woman started to scrub a floor on the little screen.

"You're trying to sell this camp thing, Bob, remember?" Art said.

"I will, I will," Bob growled at him.

John came out from behind the camera. "I've been meaning to take my kids to the zoo," he said. "They'd like to see those bat-eared foxes."

Noah told him where to find them and explained how their big ears helped to keep them cool.

Then John wanted to know where the little room with the glowing rocks was in the museum.

"OK, Bob." Art held up three fingers. "Only five minutes to wrap up the show."

Bob was ready when the last finger snapped down.

"I'm sure you've all enjoyed our guests as much as we have." The chuckle was back in his voice. "Now for a last word about Camp Tepee Town." He glanced at his notes. "The camp is a hundred miles away, near Allentown. Buses drive the boys there, and they get a chance to see some of the country. Many of these boys have never been out of the city at all. Some have never left their own neighborhoods."

"We've flown to Washington," Adam said. "For free, too."

John swung the camera around so that just the boys were on the screen.

"We found a wallet at the airport," Adam explained. "There were two tickets and boarding passes in it."

"And one thousand and two dollars," put in Noah.

"We were trying to give it all back, but the airplane took off for Washington," Adam went on.

"Skyhigh Airways flew us for free and gave us lunch," Noah said.

"Captain James is nice. He showed us how to fly the plane," Adam said. "Can we put in a plug for Skyhigh Airways?"

"I guess you just did," said Bob.

Art held up three fingers.

"I wouldn't mind going to that old camp," Adam said fast.

"Me neither," Noah said.

"Good-by, folks. Tune in tomorrow, same time." Bob smiled and chuckled.

The little screen went blank.

Bob gave a real laugh and tossed his notes aside.

"Thanks for the plug for the camp," he said.

The door of Studio II opened, and Harry and Edna crept into the room.

"I'm sorry, Bob," Harry said. "I had no idea. Honest I didn't."

"What are you sorry about, Harry? That was one of my best shows!" said Bob.

"Not much money will come in for old Tepee Town," Art said. "But I bet people will be lining up for the zoo and the Natural History Museum."

"And the airport!" Bob started to laugh again.

"We wanted to be on the screen," Adam said. "Our parents were watching. So we decided to wing it."

"You winged it, all right," said Bob. "And hogged the camera like a couple of pros — with John's help, of course. Say, did you really fly to Washington?"

Noah stood up and stretched. "I'm tired of talking now," he said. "I'm hungry." He looked at Edna.

Adam stood up and looked at Bob. "What about the ten dollars?" he said. "Harry said we'd get ten dollars."

"He did, did he?" Bob asked.

"Well, Bob, I thought that you'd be glad to —" Harry began.

"Not me, Harry," Bob said. "*You'd* be glad to."

Harry took out his wallet slowly and gave ten dollars to Adam.

"Ten dollars apiece," said Noah.

Harry glanced at Bob and even more slowly gave Noah ten dollars.

"Now," Adam said, "after lunch we'll look for a bicycle."